SANTAL FOLK TALES

By

A. CAMPBELL

Santal Folk Tales

by **A. Campbell**

ISBN: 978-93-57489-82-9

Published by

DOUBLE 9 BOOKS

2/13-B, Ansari Road, Daryaganj
New Delhi – 110002
info@double9books.com
www.double9books.com
Tel. 011-40042856

ABOUT THE AUTHOR

A. Campbell was a novelist who worked on a book with her amazing thoughts, which resulted in santal folk tales. This collection of amazing tales written by A. Campbell attempts to compile many of his classic thoughts and offer them at an affordable price, in an attractive volume so that everyone can read them. This book by A. Campbell aims to help readers understand and use Latin phrases in everyday language, particularly in legal, academic, and philosophical contexts.

CONTENTS

Preface.

Of late years the Folk tales of India have been the subject of much study and research, and several interesting collections of them have been published. But I am not aware that as yet the folk lore of the Santals, has received the attention which it deserves. The Santals as a people, have, to a remarkable degree, succeeded in resisting the subtle Hinduising influences to which they have long been exposed, and to which such a large number of aboriginal tribes have succumbed. They have retained their language, institutions, tribal organization, and religion almost intact. Their traditions show the jealousy with which these have been guarded, and the suspicion and distrust with which contact with their Aryan neighbours was regarded. The point at which they have been most accessible to outward influence and example, is in their relations with the aboriginal tribes, who in a more or less degree have merged themselves in Hinduism. Hindu ideas, customs and beliefs, filtering through these tribes, became considerably modified before they reached the Santals, and were therefore less potent in their effects than if they had been drawn from the fountain head of Hinduism itself. Still, in respect to their aboriginal neighbours they are always on their guard, ready to repel any innovation on their customs or religion with which they may be threatened. In the folk tales of such a people we may well expect to find something, if not altogether new, still interesting and instructive from an ethnological point of view, and this expectation, I believe, would be abundantly gratified if they were only made accessible to those who, by training and study, are competent to deal with them.

Santal folk-tales may be divided into two classes—those apparently purely Santal in their origin, and those obtained from other sources. Those of the first class are by far the more numerous, and besides showing the superstitious awe with which the Santals regard the creations of their own fancy, they throw a flood of light upon the social customs and usages of this most interesting people. The second class embraces a large number of the more popular tales current among the Hindus and semi-Hinduised aborigines. These, although adapted and modified by the Santals to suit their language, modes of thought, and social usages, may generally be detected by the presence of proper names, or untranslatable phrases which unmistakably indicate the source from which they have been derived.

These tales were taken down in Santali at first hand, and are therefore genuine and redolent of the soil. In translating them I have allowed myself considerable latitude without in any way diverging so far from the original as to in any degree impair their value to the student of Indian Folk-lore.

It was to be expected that in the popular tales of a simple, unpolished people like the Santals, expressions and allusions unfitted for ears polite would be found. In all such cases the changes which have been made are in accord with Santal thought and usage, so that the tales are, notwithstanding these alterations, thoroughly Santali.

I have aimed at making these Santal Folk-tales, in their English dress, true to the forests and hills of their nativity. I am not without hope, that in this I have succeeded in some small degree.

A number of the tales included in this volume have already appeared in the Indian Evangelical Review, but in this collected form they are more likely to prove of service to those who take an interest in the subject.

This volume of Santal Folk-Tales is offered as a humble contribution to the Folk-lore of India.

The Magic Lamp.

In the capital of a certain raja, there lived a poor widow. She had an only son who was of comely form and handsome countenance. One day a merchant from a far country came to her house, and standing in front of the door called out, "*dada, dada,*" (elder brother). The widow replied, "He is no more, he died many years ago." On hearing this the merchant wept bitterly, mourning the loss of his younger brother. He remained some days in his sister-in-law's house, at the end of which he said to her, "This lad and I will go in quest of the golden flowers, prepare food for our journey." Early next morning they set out taking provisions with them for the way. After they had gone a considerable distance, the boy being fatigued said, "Oh! uncle I can go no further." The merchant scolded him, and walked along as fast as he could. After some time the boy again said, "I am so tired I can go no further." His uncle turned back and beat him, and he, nerved by fear, walked rapidly along the road. At length they reached a hill, to the summit of which they climbed, and gathered a large pile of firewood. They had no fire with them, but the merchant ordered his nephew to blow with his mouth as if he were kindling the embers of a fire. He blew until he was exhausted, and then said, "What use is there in blowing when there is no fire?" The merchant replied "Blow, or I shall beat you." He again blew with all his might for a short time, and then stopping, said, "There is no fire, how can it possibly burn?" on which the merchant struck him. The lad then redoubled his efforts, and presently the pile of firewood burst into a blaze. On the firewood being consumed, an iron trap-door appeared underneath the ashes, and the merchant ordered his nephew to pull it up. He pulled, but finding himself unable to open it, said, "It will not open." The merchant told him to pull with greater force, and he, being afraid lest he should be again beaten, pulled with all his might, but could not raise it. He again said, "It will not open," whereupon the merchant struck him, and ordered him to try again. Applying himself with all his might, he at length succeeded. On the door being raised, they saw a lamp burning, and beside it an immense quantity of golden flowers.

The merchant then said to the boy, "As you enter do not touch any of the gold flowers, but put out the lamp, and heap on the gold tray as many of the gold flowers as you can, and bring them away with you." He did as he was ordered, and on reaching the door again requested his uncle to relieve him of the gold flowers, but he refused, saying, "Climb up as best as you can." The boy replied, "How can I do so, when my hands are full?" The merchant then shut the iron trap door on him, and went away to a distant country.

The boy being imprisoned in the dark vault, wept bitterly, and having no food, in a few days he became very weak. Taking the lamp in his hand, he sat down in a corner, and without knowing what he was doing, began to rub the lamp with his hand. A ring, which he wore on his finger, came into contact with the lamp, and immediately a fairy issued from it, and asked, "What is it you want with me?" He replied, "Open the door and let me out." The fairy opened the door, and the boy went home taking the lamp with him. Being hungry, he asked for food, but his mother replied, "There is nothing in the house that I can give you." He then went for his lamp, saying, "I will clean it, and then sell it, and with the money buy food." Taking the lamp in his hand he began to rub it, and his ring again touching it, a fairy issued from it and said "What do you wish for?" The boy said "Cooked rice and uncooked rice." The fairy immediately brought him an immense quantity of both kinds of rice.

Sometime after this, certain merchants brought horses for sale, and the boy seeing them wished to buy one. Having no money, he remembered his lamp, and taking it up, pressed his ring against it, and the fairy instantly appeared, and asked him what he wanted. He said, "Bring me a horse," and immediately the fairy presented to him an immense number of horses.

When the boy had become a young man, it so happened, that one day the raja's daughter was being carried to the ghat to bathe, and he seeing her palki with the attendants passing, went to his mother and said, "I am going to see the princess." She tried to dissuade him, but he insisted on her giving him permission, so at length she gave him leave. He went secretly, and saw her as she was bathing, and on returning home, said to his mother, "I have seen the princess, and I am in love with her. Go, and inform the raja that your son loves his daughter, and begs her hand in marriage." His mother said, "Do you think the raja will consider us as on an equality with him?" He would not, however, be gainsaid, but kept urging her daily to carry his message to the raja, until she being wearied with his importunity went to the palace, and being admitted to an audience, informed the raja that her son was enamoured of the princess, his daughter, and begged that she might be given to him in marriage. The raja made answer that on her son giving him a large sum of money which he named, and which would have been beyond the means of the raja himself, he would be prepared to give his daughter in marriage to her son. The young man had recourse to his lamp and ring, and the fairy supplied him with a much larger sum of money than the raja had demanded. He took it all, and gave it to the raja, who was astonished beyond measure at the sight of such immense wealth.

After a reasonable time the old mother was sent to the raja to request him to fulfil his promise, but he, being reluctant to see his daughter united to one so much her inferior in station, in hope of being relieved from the obligation to fulfil his promise, demanded that a palace suited to her rank and station in life be prepared for her, after which he would no longer delay the nuptials. The would-be bridegroom applied to his never failing friends, his lamp and ring, and on the fairy appearing begged him to build a large castle in one night, and to furnish and adorn it as befitted the residence of a raja's daughter. The fairy complied with the request, and the whole city was amazed next morning at the sight of a lordly castle, where the evening before there had not been even a hut. The dewan tried to dissuade the raja, but without effect, and in due time the marriage was celebrated amid great rejoicings.

On a certain day, some time after the marriage, the raja and his son-in-law went to the forest to hunt. During their absence, the merchant to whom reference has already been made, arrived at the castle gate, bearing in his hand a new lamp which he offered in exchange to the princess for any old lamp she might possess. She thought it a good opportunity to obtain a new lamp in place of her husband's old one, and without knowing what she did, gave the magic lamp to the merchant, and received a new one in return. The merchant rubbed his ring on the magic lamp, and the fairy obeyed the summons, and desired to know what he wanted. He said, "Convey the castle as it stands with the princess in it, to my own country," and instantly his wish was gratified.

When the raja and his son-in-law returned from the chase, they were surprised and alarmed to find that the palace with its fair occupant had vanished, and had not left a trace behind. The dewan reminded his master that he had tried to dissuade him from rashly giving his daughter in marriage to an unknown person, and had foretold that some calamity was sure to follow. The raja being grieved and angry at the loss of his daughter, sent for her husband, and said to him, "I give you thirteen days during which to find my daughter. If you fail, on the morning of the fourteenth, I shall surely cause you to be executed." The thirteenth day arrived, and although her husband had sought her every where, the princess had not been found. Her unhappy husband resigned himself to his fate, saying, "I shall go and rest, to-morrow morning I shall be killed." So he climbed to the top of a high hill, and lay down to sleep upon a rock. At noon he accidentally rubbed his finger ring upon the rock on which he lay, and a fairy issued from it, and awaking him, demanded what he wanted. In reply he said, "I have lost my wife and my palace, if you know where they are, take me to them." The fairy immediately transported him to the gate of his castle in the merchant's country, and then left him to his own devices. Assuming the form of a dog, he entered the palace, and the princess at once recognized him. The merchant had gone out on business, and had taken the lamp with him, suspended by a chain round his neck. After consultation, it was determined that the princess should put poison in the merchant's food that evening. When he returned, he called for his supper, and the princess set before him the poisoned rice, after eating which he quickly died. The rightful owner repossessed himself of the magic lamp, and an application of the ring brought out the attendant fairy who demanded to know why he had been summoned. "Transport my castle with the princess and myself in it back to the king's country, and place it where it stood before," said the young man; and instantly the castle occupied its former position. So that before the morning of the fourteenth day dawned, not only had the princess been found, but her palace had been restored to its former place. The raja was delighted at receiving his daughter back again. He divided his kingdom with his son-in-law, giving him one-half, and they ruled the country peacefully and prosperously for many years.

The Two Brothers, Jhorea, and Jhore.

There were two brothers, whose parents died, leaving them orphans when very young. The name of the elder was Jhorea, and of the younger Jhore. On the death of their parents, the two brothers went to seek employment, which they found in a certain village, far from where their home had been. The elder, Jhorea, was engaged as a farm servant, and the younger, Jhore, as village goat-herd.

After some time, it so happened that one day the brothers had no rice for their dinner, and Jhorea said to his brother, "Go to the owners of the goats you herd, and ask them for the hire they promised you. One will give you a *pai*, another a *pawa*, and a third a *paila*, and so on, according to the number of animals they have in your charge; some will give you more and others less, bring what you get, and cook some for dinner." The boy went as he was ordered, and entering the first house he came to, said, "Give me a *pai*." They said: "What do you want with a *pai*?" "Never mind what I want with it, give it," he replied. So they gave him a *pai*. Then he went to another house and said, "Give me a *pawa*." "What do you want with a *pawa*?" they said. "Never you mind, give it to me," and they gave him a *pawa*. He then went to a third house and asked for a *paila*. "What do you want with a *paila*?" they enquired. "Never you mind, give it to me," he replied. Instead of bringing rice he brought the wooden measures, and breaking them into small pieces, put them into the pot to cook. The elder brother was ploughing, and being very hungry, he kept calling out, "Cook the rice quickly, cook the rice quickly." His brother being impatient, he stirred the contents of the pot with all his might, at the same time exclaiming, "What can be the matter brother? it is very hard." The elder brother came to see what was wrong, and on looking into the pot saw only pieces of wood. He became very angry, and said, "I sent you to bring rice, why did you bring measures?" To which he replied, "You told me to ask a *pai* from one, a *pawa* from another, and a *paila* from a third, and I did so."

The elder then said to the younger, "You go and plough, and if the plough catch in a root on the right hand, cut the root on the left hand, and if it catch in a root on the left side, cut the root on the right side, and in the meantime I will cook." He went and began to plough, and in a short time the plough caught in a root on the right, and not understanding the directions given to him, he struck the left hand bullock a blow on the leg with his axe. The bullock limped along a short distance. When the plough caught in a root on the left, he smote the bullock on the right, wounding it as he had done the other. Both of the bullocks then lay down, and although he beat them they did not get up. He therefore called to his brother, "These bullocks have lain down, and will not get up, what shall I do?" "Beat them," was the reply. Again he beat them, but with no better result. The elder brother then came, and found that the oxen had been maimed, and were unable to stand, at which he became greatly alarmed, and said, "Why did you maim the oxen? The owners will beat us to death to-day." He then gave him some parched grain to eat, and sent him to look after his goats. The sun being hot, the goats were lying in the shade chewing their cud. He sat down near them, and began to eat the parched grain. Seeing the goats moving their jaws as if eating, he said, "These goats are eating nothing, they are lying there mocking me," and becoming enraged, he killed them all with his axe. Then going to his brother, he said, "Oh! brother, I have killed all the goats." His brother asked, "Why did you kill them?" He replied, "While I was watching them and eating the parched grain which you gave me, I saw them chewing, and as they were eating nothing I knew they were mocking me, and so I killed them all." The elder brother became greatly alarmed, and calling to the younger to come, they quickly ate their dinner, and then went to where the goats were lying dead. From among them they chose the fattest, and carried it off to the jungle, where they flayed, and cut it into pieces.

Jhore then said, "I shall take the stomach as my share," but his brother said, "No, let us take the flesh." Jhore, however, would not agree to that, and at length his brother said, "Well you take the stomach, I shall take the flesh." So each took what he fancied most, and they set off. After travelling a long distance, they came to a large tree growing on the side of the road, into which they climbed for safety. After they had been some time on the tree, a raja on his way to be married, lay down to rest in its shade, and when he and his attendants had fallen asleep, Jhore let the goat's stomach fall down on the raja. The raja having his rest thus rudely disturbed, sprang to his feet, and calling out, awoke his servants, who seeing the goat's stomach, and not knowing what had happened, thought the raja himself had burst. They fled in terror followed by the raja, and did not halt till they were many miles away from the scene of the raja's discomfiture.

After waiting a little while, the brothers descended, and began to help themselves to the raja's property. Jhore said, "I shall take the drum." His brother said, "No, let us take the brass vessels and the clothes." Jhore, however, insisted, and after considerable wrangling, his brother said, "Well, take the drum if you will have it, I shall take the brass vessels and the clothes." So each took what pleased him best, and then they went away and hid in the jungle.

While walking about in the jungle, they collected bees, wasps, and other stinging insects, and put them into the drum. Having filled the drum, they emerged from the forest at a place where a washerman was washing clothes. Jhore tore all his clothes into strips, and scattered them about. The washerman went and told the raja that two persons had come out from the jungle, and had destroyed all his clothes. On hearing this, the raja said to his servants, "Come, and let us fight with these two men." So arming themselves with guns, they went to the tank where Jhorea and Jhore were sitting, and began to shoot at them, but the bullets did them no harm. When their ammunition was exhausted, they said, "Will you still fight?" The brothers answered, "Yes, we will fight." So they began to fire their guns, and beat their drum, and the bees and wasps issued from it like a rope, and began to sting the raja and his soldiers, who to save themselves, lay down and rolled on the ground. The raja, in anguish from the stings of the bees, exclaimed, "I will give you my daughter, and half of my kingdom, if you will call off the bees." Hearing this they beat the drum, and calling to the bees and wasps, ordered them all to enter the drum again, and the raja and his people went to their homes. The brothers however, could not agree as to who should marry the princess. One said, "You marry her." The other said, "No, you marry her." The younger at length said to the elder, "You are the elder, you should take her, as it is not fitting that you should beg. If I were to marry her, I could no longer go about begging." So the elder brother married the princess, and became the raja's son-in-law.

The two settled down there, and cultivated all kinds of crops. One day the elder brother sent his younger brother to bring a certain kind of grain. Taking a sickle and a rope to tie his sheaves with, he went to the field. Arrived there, he found that the grain was covered with insects. So he set fire to it, and while it was burning he kept calling out, "Whoever desires to feast on roasted insects, let him come here." When his brother knew what he had done, he reprimanded him severely.

Some time afterwards, when the black rice was ripe, he again ordered him to go and reap some, so getting a sickle, and rope to bind his sheaves with, he went to the rice field. On looking about to see where he would begin, he discovered that each stalk of rice was covered with flies. "There is nothing here but flies. How can I reap this?" Saying this, he set fire to the growing rice and burnt it all to the ground. His brother, when he knew what had happened, was very much displeased and threatened to beat him.

On another day he was sent to cut *jari* 1 to make ropes, so taking his sickle, he set off to the field of *jari*. As soon as he began to cut the stalks, the seeds rattled in the pods, hearing which he stopped and called out, "Who is calling me?" After listening awhile and hearing nothing he began again, and the same noise issuing from the plant he was cutting, he said, "These plants are remonstrating with me for cutting them." So being offended, he set fire to and burnt down the whole crop of *jari*.

On being informed of his brother's action, Jhorea seized a stick, and ran after him to beat him, but could not overtake him. In the direction Jhore was running, there were some men flaying an ox, and Jhorea called to them to lay hold of his brother. They could not, however, accomplish this, but as he passed, they threw the stomach of the ox at him, which he caught in his arms and carried away with him. Finding a drain that was open at both ends, he crept in at one end, and passed out at the other, but left the ox's stomach behind him. His brother soon arrived at the drain, and thinking he was still there, tried to drive him out by pushing in a stick, the sharp point of which perforated the ox's stomach. On withdrawing the stick, and seeing the contents of the ox's stomach adhering to it, he thought he had pierced and killed his brother, but he having passed out at the other end had run swiftly home, and hid himself among the rafters of the house. Jhorea returned home weeping, and immediately began to make the preparations necessary for Jhore's funeral ceremonies. He caused a sumptuous feast to be got ready, and invited all his relations and friends. When they were all assembled, he went into the house to offer Jhore his portion. Presenting it, he said: "Oh! my brother Jhore, I offer this to you, take it, and eat it." Jhore, from among the rafters said, "Give it to me brother, and I shall eat it." His brother, not expecting an answer, was alarmed, and fled to his friends without, exclaiming, "Do the spirits of dead men speak? Jhore's speaks."

It now being dark, Jhore descended from his perch, and taking up the food which had been cooked for his funeral feast, left the house by another door. Passing on to the high way, he kept calling out, "Travellers by the road, or dwellers in the jungle, if you require food, come here." Some thieves hearing him, said, "Come, let us go and ask some." So going to him they said, "Give us some too, Jhore." But he replied, "It is for me alone." On their asking a second time, he give it to them. After they had eaten it all, they said to him, "Come, let us go a thieving." So they went to a house, and while the thieves were searching for money, Jhore went and picked up small pieces of pottery, and tied them up in his cloth. When they met afterwards, seeing Jhore's bundle of what appeared like rupees, they said, "You were not with us, where did you get the money?" Opening his parcel, he shewed them the pieces of pottery, seeing which they said, "We will not have you as our comrade." He replied, "Then return the food which you ate." As they could not comply, they agreed to take him with them. Jhore then said, "Where shall we go now?" They replied, "To steal cloth." So they went to a house, and while the robbers were searching for cloth, Jhore began to pull the clothes from off the sleeping inmates. This awoke them, and starting up, they began to call loudly for help. The thieves made off, and Jhore with them. Seeing Jhore had spoiled their game, they said to him, "We will not allow you to go with us again." He said, "Then give me back the food you ate." Not being able to do so, they said, "Well, we will allow you to accompany us this once." Jhore then said, "What shall we steal now?" The thieves answered, "We shall now go to steal horses." So they went to a stable, and each of the thieves helped himself to a horse; but Jhore going behind the house, found a large tiger which he saddled and mounted. The thieves also mounted each on the horse he had stolen. As they rode along, Jhore's tiger sometimes went first, and sometimes the thieves' horses. When the thieves were in front, Jhore's tiger bit and scratched their horses, so they said to him, "You ride first, we shall follow." But Jhore said, "No, my horse is a Hindu horse, he cannot run in front, your horses are Santal horses, they run well and straight, so you ride ahead." When day began to dawn, Jhore's tiger evinced a tendency to leave the road and take to the jungle, but Jhore holding him in, exclaimed, "Ha! ha! my Hindu steed, ha! ha! my Hindu steed." When it was fully light, the tiger ran into the jungle, and Jhore got caught in the branch of a tree, and continued dangling there for some days.

It so happened that one morning a demon passing that way spied Jhore dangling from the tree, and seizing him, put him in a bag and carried him away. Being thirsty, he laid the bag down, and went to a spring to drink. While he was absent, Jhore got out of the bag, and putting a stone in instead, ran away. The demon having quenched his thirst, returned, and lifting the bag carried it home. His daughter came to welcome him, and he said to her, "Jhore is in the bag, cook him, and we shall have a feast." He then went to invite his friends to share it with him. When the demon's daughter had opened the bag, she found the stone, and was angry, because her father had deceived her. In a short time her father returned, bringing a large number of jackals with him. He said to her, "Have you cooked Jhore?" She replied, "Tush! tush! you brought me a stone."

The demon was highly incensed at having been outwitted, and exclaimed, "I will track Jhore till I find him, and this time I shall bring him home without laying him down." He then left, and before long found Jhore swinging in the same branch as before. Catching hold of him, he put him into a bag, the mouth of which he tied. This time he brought him home without once laying him down. Calling to his daughter, he said, "Cook Jhore, while I go to invite my friends." She untied the bag, and took Jhore out, and seeing his long hair, she said, "How is it that your hair has grown so long?" "I pounded it in the dhenki," he replied, "Will you pound mine, so that it may become long like yours," said the demon's daughter. Jhore replied, "I shall do so with pleasure, put your head in the dhenki, and I shall pound it." So she put in her head, and he pounded it so that he killed her. He then possessed himself of all her jewellery, and dressing in her clothes, cooked her body.

When the demon returned, accompanied by his friends, he said, "Well! daughter, have you cooked Jhore?" Jhore replied, "Yes, I have cooked him." On hearing this, the demon and the jackals who had come with him, were delighted, and setting to, they devoured the body of the demon's daughter.

After some days, the demon went to visit a friend, and Jhore divesting himself of the demon girl's clothes, went to where the demon had at first found him, and began to swing as before. Presently a tigress approached him and said, "Oh! brother, the hair of my cubs has grown very long, I wish you to shave them to-day." Jhore replied, "Oh! sister, boil some water, and then go to the spring to bring more." The tigress having boiled the water, went to the spring. While she was away, Jhore poured the boiling water over the two cubs, and scalded them to death. He made them grin by fixing the lips apart, and propped them up at the door of the tigress' house. On her return as she drew near, she saw her cubs, as she fancied, laughing, and said to herself. "They are delighted because their uncle has shaved them." Setting down her water pot, she went to look at them, and found them dead. Just then the demon came up, and she asked him, "Whom are you seeking to-day uncle?" He replied "I am seeking Jhore, he has caused me to eat my own daughter. Whom are you seeking?" The tigress replied, "I also am seeking Jhore; he has scalded my cubs to death."

The two then went in search of Jhore. They found him in a lonely part of the forest preparing birdlime, and said to him, "What are you doing, Jhore?" He replied, "I look high up, and then I look deep down." They said, "Teach us to do it too." He answered, "Only I can do it." They asked him a second time, and received the same reply. On their begging him a third time to teach them, he said, "Well, I shall do it." He then put some of the birdlime into their eyes, and fixed their eyelids together, so that they could not open them. While they were washing their eyes, he ran away. As soon as they had rid themselves of the birdlime, they followed him and found him distilling oil from the fruit of the marking-nut tree. They said to him, "What are you doing, Jhore?" He replied, "I look deep down, and then high up." They said, "Teach us also." He replied, "Only I can do it." They asked him again, and he said, "Well I will do it." He then poured some of the oil he had distilled into their eyes. It burned them so, that they became stone-blind.

Jhore was next seen seated in a fig-tree eating the fruit. Some cattle merchants, passing under the tree with a large herd of cattle, saw him eating the figs, and asked him what it was he was eating. He replied, "Beat the bullock that is going last, and you shall find it." So they beat the bullock till it fell down. In the meantime, the herd had gone on ahead, and Jhore running after them drove them to his own house. His brother seeing the large herd of cattle, asked to whom they belonged. Jhore replied, "They are Jhore's property." Jhorea then said, "I killed my brother Jhore, what Jhore is it?" He made answer, "Your brother Jhore whom you thought you had killed." Jhorea was delighted to find his brother alive, and said to him, "Let us live together after this." So they lived peacefully together ever after.

1 *Jari* is the Santali name for *Crotalaria Juncea*, a fibre yielding plant the seeds of which when ripe, rattle in the pods when the plant is shaken.

The Boy and his Stepmother.

A certain boy had charge of a cow which he used to tend while grazing. One day the cow said to him, "How is it that you are becoming so emaciated?" The boy replied, "My stepmother does not give me sufficient food." The cow then said to him, "Do not tell any one, and I will give you food. Go to the jungle and get leaves with which to make a plate and cup." The boy did as he was ordered, and behold, the cow from one horn shook boiled rice into the leaf plate, and from the other a relish for the rice into the cup. This continued daily for a considerable time, until the boy became sleek and fat.

The stepmother came to know of the relation which existed between the cow and her herd-boy, and to be revenged upon them she feigned illness. To her attendants she said, "I cannot possibly live." They asked, "What would make you live?" She replied, "If you kill the cow, I will recover." They said, "If killing the cow will cure you, we will kill it." The boy hearing that the life of the cow which supplied him with food was threatened, ran to her and said, "They are about to kill you." Hearing this the cow said, "You go and make a rope of rice straw, make some parts thick, and some thin, and put it in such a place as they can easily find it. When they are about to kill me, you seize hold of my tail and pull." The next day they proceeded to make arrangements to kill the cow, and finding the rope prepared by the boy the day before, they tied her with it to a stake. After she was tied the boy laid hold of her tail, and pulled so that the rope by which she was secured was made taut. A man now raised an axe, and felled her by a blow on the forehead. As the cow staggered the rope broke, and she and the boy were borne away on the wind, and alighted in an unexplored jungle. From the one cow other cows sprang, in number equal to a large herd, and from them another large herd was produced. The boy then drove his two herds of cows to a place where they could graze, and afterwards took them to the river to drink. The cows having quenched their thirst, lay down to rest, and the boy bathed, and afterwards combed and dressed his hair. During this latter operation a hair from his head fell into the river, and was carried away by the current.

Some distance lower down, a princess with her female companions and attendants came to bathe. While the princess was in the water she noticed the hair floating down stream, and ordered some one to take it out, which when done they measured, and found it to be twelve cubits long. The princess on returning home went to the king, her father, and showing him the hair she had found in the river said, "I have made up my mind to marry the man to whom this hair belonged." The king gave his consent, and commanded his servants to search for the object of his daughter's affection. They having received the king's command went to a certain barber and said to him, "You dress the hair and beards of all the men in this part of the country, tell us where the man with hair twelve cubits long is to be found." The barber, after many days, returned unsuccessful. The king's servants after a long consultation as to whom they should next apply to, decided upon laying the matter before a tame parrot belonging to the king. Going to the parrot they said, "Oh parrot, can you find the man whose hair is twelve cubits long?" The parrot replied, "Yes, I can find him." After flying here and there the parrot was fortunate enough to find the boy. It was evening, and having driven his two herds of cattle into their pen, he had sat down, and was employed in dressing his long hair. His flute was hanging on a bush by his side.

The parrot sat awhile considering how she might take him to the king's palace. Seeing the flute the idea was suggested to her, that by means of it she might contrive to lead him where she desired. So taking it up in her beak, she flew forward a little and alighted in a small bush. To regain possession of his flute the boy followed, but on his approach the bird flew away, and alighted on another bush a short distance ahead. In this way she continued to lead him by flying from bush to bush until at length she brought him to the king's palace. He was then brought before his majesty, and his hair measured, and found to be twelve cubits in length. The king then ordered food to be set before him, and after he was refreshed the betrothal ceremony was performed.

As it was now late they prevailed upon him to pass the night as the guest of the king. Early in the morning he set out, but, as he had a long distance to go, the day was far advanced before he reached the place where his cattle were. They were angry at having been kept penned up to so late an hour, and as he removed the bars to let them out, they knocked him down, and trampled upon his hair in such a way, as to pull it all out leaving him bald. Nothing daunted, he collected his cows, and started on his return journey, but us he drove them along, one after another vanished, so that only a few remained when he reached the king's palace.

On his arrival they noticed that he had lost all his hair, and on being questioned he related to the king all that had fallen him. His hair being gone the princess refused to marry him, so instead of becoming the king's son-in-law, he became one of his hired servants.

The Story of Kara and Guja.

There were two brothers named Kara and Guja. Guja, who was the elder did the work at home, and Kara was ploughman.

One day the two went to the forest to dig edible roots. After they had been thus engaged for some hours, Kara said to Guja, "Look up and see the sun's position in the heavens." Looking up he said, "Oh brother, one is rising and another is setting." They then said, "The day is not yet past, let us bestir ourselves, and lose no time." So they dug with all their might.

After digging a long time Kara looked up and became aware that it was night. He then exclaimed, "Oh brother, it is now night, what shall we do? Come let us seek some place where we can remain until the morning." After they had wandered awhile in the forest they spied a light in the distance, and on drawing near they found that a tiger had kindled a fire, and was warming himself. Going up to the entrance to the cave they called out to the tiger, "Oh uncle, give us a place to sleep in." He answered, "Come in." So the two went in, and being hungry began to roast and eat the roots they had brought with them. The tiger hearing them eating, enquired what it was. They replied, "Oh uncle, we are roasting and eating the roots which we dug up in the forest." He then said, "Oh my nephews, I will also try how they taste." So they handed him a piece of charcoal, and as he munched it he said, "Oh my nephews, how is it that I feel it grating between my teeth?" They replied, "It is an old one that you have got, uncle." He then said, "Give me another, and I will try it." So they gave him another piece of charcoal, and after he had crunched it awhile he said, "Oh my nephews, this is as bad as the other," to which they rejoined, "Oh uncle, your mouth is old, therefore what is good to us, is the reverse to you." The tiger did not wish to try his grinders on another piece of charcoal, so the brothers were left to enjoy their repast alone.

After they had eaten all the roots, Guja said to Kara, "What shall we eat now? Come let us eat this old tiger's tail." Kara replied, "Do not talk in that way, brother, the tiger will devour us." "Not so, brother," said Guja, "I have a great desire to eat flesh." The old tiger understood their conversation, and being afraid tried to get out of the cave, but the brothers caught hold of him, and wrenched off his tail, which they roasted in the ashes, and then ate.

The tiger after losing his tail summoned a council of all the tigers inhabiting that part of the forest, at which they decided to kill and eat the two brothers. So they went to the cave, but Kara and Guja had fled, and had taken refuge in a palm tree which grew on the edge of a large deep tank. Not finding them in the cave the tigers, headed by him who had lost his tail, went in quest of them, and coming to the tank saw them reflected in the water, and one after another they dived in, thinking they would be able to seize them, but of course they could not catch a shadow. One of the tigers, when in the act of yawning, looked upwards, and seeing them in the tree exclaimed, "There they are. There they are." They then asked the brothers how they had managed to climb up, to which they replied, "We stood on each other's shoulders." The tigers then said, "Come, let us do the same, and we shall soon reach them." As the tailless tiger was most interested in their capture, they made him stand lowest, and a tiger climbed up and stood on his shoulders, and another on his, and so on; but before they reached the brothers, Kara called out to Guja, "Give me your sharp battle-axe, and I shall hamstring the tailless tiger." The tailless tiger forgetting himself jumped to one side, and the whole pillar of tigers fell in a heap on the ground. They now began to abuse the old tailless tiger, who fearing lest they should tear him in pieces fled into the forest.

After the tigers had left, the two brothers descended from the palm tree, and walked rapidly away as they dreaded that the tigers might yet follow them. Towards evening they came to a village, and entering into the house of an old woman lay down to sleep. The owner of the house observing them said, "Oh my children, do not sleep to-night, for there is a demon who visits in rotation each house in the village, and each time he comes carries off some one and eats him; it is my turn to receive a visit to-night." They said, "Do not trouble us now, let us sleep, as we are tired." So they slept, but kept their weather eye open. During the night the old woman came quietly, and began to bite their arms, which they had laid aside before retiring to rest. Hearing a sound as if some one were crunching iron between his teeth, the brothers called out, "Old woman, what are you eating?" She replied "Only a few roasted peas which I brought from the chief's house." About midnight the demon came, and as he was entering the house Kara and Guja shot at him with their bows and arrows, and he fell down dead. Then they cut out his claws and tongue, and placed them in a bag. Afterwards they threw out the body of the demon into the garden behind the house.

Now it so happened that the king had promised to give his daughter and half of his kingdom to the man who should slay the demon. Early in the morning a Dome, who was passing, discovered the body of the demon, and said within himself, "I will take it to the king and claim the reward." So running home he broke all the furniture in his house and beat his old woman saying, "Get out of this. I am about to bring the king's daughter home as my bride." He then returned quickly, and taking up the body of the demon carried it to the king, and said, "Oh sir king, I have slain the demon." The king replied, "Very well, we will enquire into it." So he commanded some of his servants to examine the body, and on doing so they found that the claws had been extracted and the tongue cut out. They reported the condition of the body to the king, who ordered the Dome to state the weapon with which he killed him. The Dome replied, "I hit him with a club on the head." On the head being examined no mark whatever was seen, so in order to arrive at the truth the king ordered all the inhabitants of the village to be brought together to the palace. He then enquired of them as to who killed the demon.

The old woman, in whose house Kara and Guja had passed the night, stepped forward and said, "Oh sir king, two strangers came to my house yesterday evening, and during the night they slew the demon." The king said, "Where are those two men?" The old woman replied, "There they are, the two walking together." So the king sent and brought them back, and questioned them as to the slaying of the demon. They pointed out the arrow-marks on the body, and produced his claws and tongue from their bag. This evidence convinced the king that they, and not the Dome, had slain the demon. Kara and Guja were received with great favour by the king, and received the promised reward.

The king sentenced the Dome to be beaten and driven from the village. After receiving his stripes, the Dome returned home, and gathered the shreds of his property together. He also went in search of his Dome wife and children, but they mocked him saying, "You went to marry the king's daughter, why do you come again seeking us."

Thus Kara and Guja gained a kingdom.

The King and his inquisitive Queen.

There was a certain king known by the name of Huntsman, on account of his expertness in the chase. One day when returning from the forest where he had been hunting he found a serpent and a lizard fighting on the path along which he was moving. As they were blocking the way he ordered them to stand aside and allow him to pass, but they gave no heed to what he said. King Huntsman then began to beat them with his staff. He killed the lizard, but the serpent fled, and so escaped.

The serpent then went to Monsha, the king of the serpents, and complained of the treatment the lizard and himself had received at the hands of king Huntsman. The next day king Monsha went and met king Huntsman on his way home from the forest, and blocked his way so that he could not pass. King Huntsman being angry said, "Clear the way, and allow me to pass, or else I shall send an arrow into you. Why do you block my way?" King Monsha replied, "Why did you assault the lizard and the serpent, with intent to kill them both?" King Huntsman answered, "I ordered them to get out of my way, but they would not, I therefore assaulted them, and killed one. The other saved himself by flight." King Monsha hearing this explanation said, "Very good, the fault was theirs, not yours."

King Huntsman then petitioned the king of the serpents to bestow upon him the gift of understanding the language of animals and insects. King Monsha acceded to his request, and gave him the gift he desired.

A few days after this event King Huntsman went to the forest, and after hunting all day returned home in the evening Having washed his hands and feet, he sat down to his meal of boiled rice. When the rice was being served to the king a few grains fell on the ground, and a fly and an ant began to dispute as to who should carry them away. The fly said, "I will take them to my children." The ant replied, "No, I will take them to mine." Hearing the two talk thus, the king was amused, and began to smile. The queen, who was standing by, said to him, "Tell me what has made you laugh." On being thus addressed the king became greatly confused, for at the time the gift of understanding the language of animals and insects was bestowed upon him, King Monsha had forbidden him to make it known to any one. He had said, "If you tell this to any one, I shall eat you." Remembering this the king feared to answer the question put to him by the queen. He tried to deceive her by saying, "I did not laugh, you must have been mistaken." She would not, however, be thus put off, so the king was obliged to tell her that if he answered her question his life would be forfeited. The queen was inexorable, and said, "Whether you forfeit your life or not, you must tell me." The king then said, "Well, if it must be so, let us make ready to go to the bank of the Ganges. There I shall tell you, and when I have done so you must push me into the river, and then return home."

The king armed himself, and the two set out for the river. When they had reached it, they sat down to rest under the shade of a tree. A flock of goats was grazing near to where they were seated, and the king's attention was arrested by a conversation which was being carried on between an old she-goat and a young he-goat. The former addressed the latter thus, "There is an island in the middle of the Ganges, and on that island there is a large quantity of good sweet grass. Get the grass for me, and I shall give you my daughter in marriage." The he-goat was not thus to be imposed upon. He angrily addressed his female friend as follows, "Do not think to make me like this foolish king, who vainly tries to please a woman. He has come here to lose his own life at the bidding of one. You tell me to go and bring you grass out of such a flood as this. I am no such fool. I do not care to die yet. There are many more quite as good as your daughter."

The king understood what passed between them, and admitted to himself the truth of what the he-goat had said. After considering a short time he arose, and having made a rude sacrificial altar, said to the queen, "Kneel down, and do me obeisance, and I shall tell you what made me laugh." She knelt down, and the king struck off her head and burnt her body upon the altar. Returning home he performed her funeral ceremonies, after which he married another wife.

He reigned prosperously for many years, and decided all disputes that were brought before him by animals or insects.

The Story of Bitaram.

In a certain village there lived seven brothers. The youngest of them planted a certain vegetable, and went every day to examine it to see how it was growing. For a long time there were only the stalk and leaves, but at length a flower appeared, and from it a fruit. This fruit he measured daily to mark its growth. It grew continuously until it became exactly a span long, after which it remained stationary. One day he said to his sisters-in-law, "Do not eat my fruit, for whoever does so will give birth to a child only one span long." He continued his daily visits to his plant as usual, and was pleased to note that the fruit was evidently ripening. One day, during his absence, one of his sisters-in-law plucked the fruit and ate it. On returning from the field where he had been ploughing, he went to look at and measure his fruit, but it was gone, it had been stolen. Suspecting that some one of his sisters-in-law was the thief, he accused each of them in turn, but they all denied having touched it. When he found that no one would confess to having taken it, he said to them, "Do not tell upon yourselves, the thief will be caught before long." And so it happened, for one of them gave birth to a baby one span long. The first time he saw his sister-in-law after the child was born he laughed, and said to her, "You denied having stolen my fruit, now you see I have found you out."

When the time came that the child should receive a name, Bitaram1 was given to him, because he was only a span in height. Bitaram's mother used to take food to the brothers to the field when they were ploughing, and when Bitaram was able to walk so far he accompanied her. One day he surprised his mother by saying, "Let me take the food to my father and uncles to-day." She replied, "What a fancy! You, child, are only a span high, how can you carry it?" But Bitaram insisted saying, "I can carry it well enough, and carry it I will." His mother being unable to resist his pertinacity said, "Then, child, take it, and be off." So she placed the basket on his head and he set out. Arrived at the field he went up a furrow, but the ground was so uneven that before he reached his destination, he had lost nearly all the rice, which had been shaken out of the basket. On his coming near, one of his uncles called out, "Is that you Bitaram?" He replied, "Yes, it is I, Bitaram." Climbing up out of the furrow, he put down the basket saying, "Help yourselves, and I will take the oxen and buffaloes to the water." So saying, he drove off the cattle to the river. When they had quenched their thirst he gathered them together, and began to drive them back again to where he had left his father and uncles. While following them up the sandy back of the river, he fell into a depression made by the hoof of a buffalo, and was soon covered up by the loose sand sent rolling down by the herd as they ascended.

When the cattle returned without Bitaram, his father and uncles became alarmed for his safety, and immediately went in search of him. They went here and there calling out "Bitaram, where are you?" But failing to find him they concluded that he had been devoured by some wild animal, and returned sorrowfully home. Rain fell during the night, and washed the sand from off Bitaram, so that he was able to get up, and climb out. On his way home he encountered some thieves who were dividing their booty in a lonely part of the forest. Bitaram hearing them disputing called out "*Kehe kere*" at the pitch of his voice. The thieves hearing the sound, looked round on all sides to see who was near, but the night being dark, and they not directing their eyes near enough to the ground to see Bitaram, they could discern no one. Then they said to each other, "Let us seek safety in flight. A spirit has been sent to watch us." So they all made off leaving behind them the brass vessels they had stolen. Bitaram gathered these up, and hid them among some prickly bushes, and then went home.

It was now past midnight, and all had retired to rest, and as Bitaram stood shivering with cold at the closed door, he called out, "Open the door and let me in." His father hearing him said, "Is that you Bitaram?" He replied, "Yes, open the door." They then enquired where he had been, and he related all that had happened to him after he had driven the cattle to the river. Having warmed himself at the fire, he told his father of his adventure with the thieves in the forest. He said, "I despoiled some thieves, whom I met in the jungle, of the brass vessels they had stolen." His father replied, "Foolish child, do not tell lies, you yourself are not the height of a brass *lota*" (drinking-cup). "No father," said Bitaram, "I am telling the truth, come and I will shew you where they are." His father and uncles went with him, and he pointed out to them the vessels hidden among the prickly bushes. They picked them all up and brought them home.

Early next morning some sepoys, who were searching for the thieves, happened to pass that way, and seeing the stolen property lying out side of the house, recognized it, and apprehended Bitaram's father and uncles and dragged them off to prison. After this Bitaram and his mother were obliged to beg their bread from house to house. She often attributed to him the misery which had befallen them, saying, "Had it not been for your pertinacity, your father and uncles would not have been deprived of their liberty."

One day, as they were following their usual avocation, they entered a certain house, and Bitaram said to his mother, "Ask the people of the house to give me a *tumki*.2" She did not at first comply, but he kept urging her until being irritated she said, "It was through your pertinacity in insisting upon being allowed to carry the food to your father and uncles that they are now bound and in prison, and yet you will not give up the bad habit." Bitaram said, "No, mother, do ask it for me." As he would not be silenced she begged it for him, and the people kindly gave it.

At the next house they came to, they saw a cat walking about, and Bitaram said, "Oh mother, ask the people to give me the cat." As before, she at first refused, but he continued to press her, and she becoming annoyed scolded him saying, "The young gentleman insists on obtaining this and that. It was your pertinacity that caused your father and uncles to be dragged to prison in bonds." Bitaram replied, "Not so, mother, do ask them to give me the cat." As the only way to silence him she said to the people of the house, "Give my boy your cat, he will hold it in his arms for a few minutes, and then set it down, but he carried it away with him." Bitaram then begged his mother to make him a bag, and fill it with flour, saying, "I am going to obtain the release of my father and uncles." She mockingly replied, "Much you can do." She made him a bag, however, and filling it with flour said, "Be off."

Bitaram then strapped the bag of flour on the cat's back as a saddle, and mounted. Puss, however, refused to go in the direction desired, and it was with great difficulty that he prevailed upon her to take the road. As he rode along he observed a swarm of bees on an ant hill, and dismounting he addressed them as follows, "Come bees, go in, come bees, go in." The bees swarmed into the *tumki*, and Bitaram having covered them up with a leaf continued his journey. Before he had gone far he came to a large tank, which belonged to the raja who had imprisoned his father. A number of women had come to the tank for water, and Bitaram taking his stand upon the embankment began to shoot arrows at their waterpots. After he had broken several, the women espied him mounted on his cat with his bow and arrows in his hand, and believing him to be an elf from the forest fled in terror to the city. Going to the raja they said "Oh raja, come and see. Some one is on the tank embankment. We do not know who or what he is, but he is only a span high." The raja then summoned his soldiers, and commanded them to take their bows and arrows, and go and shoot him whoever he was. The soldiers went within range, but although they shot away all their arrows, they failed to hit him. So returning to the raja they said, "He cannot be shot." Hearing this the raja became angry, and calling for his bow and arrows, went to the tank and began to shoot at Bitaram, but although he persevered until his right side ached with drawing the bow, he could not hit him.

When he desisted, Bitaram called out "Are you exhausted?" The raja answered "Yes." Then said Bitaram "It is my turn now," and taking the leaf from off the mouth of the basket called to the bees, "Go into the battle, bees." The bees issued from the basket like a black rope, and stung the raja and those who were with him. No way of escape offering, the raja called out to Bitaram, "Call off your bees, and I will give you the half of my kingdom and my daughter, and I will also set at liberty your father and uncles." Bitaram gathered the bees into the basket, and after his father and uncles had been released, took them back to the ant hill from whence he had brought them. On his return he wedded the princess and received half of her father's kingdom.

Bitaram and his wife lived happily together, and every thing they took in hand prospered, so that before long they were richer than the king himself. One great source of Bitaram's wealth was a cow which the princess had brought him as part of her dowry. Being envious of their good fortune, the raja and his sons resolved to kill the cow, and thus obtain possession of all the gold and silver. So they put the cow to death, but when they had cut her up they were disappointed as neither gold nor silver were found in her stomach.

Bitaram placed his cow's hide in the sun, and when it was dry carried it away to sell it. Darkness coming on he climbed into a tree for safety, as wild beasts infested the forest through which he was passing. During the night some thieves came under the tree in which he was, and began to divide the money they had stolen. Bitaram then relaxed his hold of the dry hide, which made such a noise as it fell from branch to branch that the thieves fled terror-stricken, and left all their booty behind them. In the morning Bitaram descended, and collecting all the rupees carried them home. He then shewed the money to his wife, and said "Go and ask the loan of your father's *paila*, that I may measure them." So she went and brought the measure, which had several cracks in it. Having measured his money he sent back the raja's *paila*, but he had not noticed that one or two pieces were left sticking in the cracks. So they said to him, "Where did you get the money?" He replied "By the sale of my cow's hide." Hearing this they said, "Will the merchant who bought yours, buy any more?" He said, "Yes. I received all this money for my one hide, how much more may not you receive seeing you have such large herds of cattle! If you dispose of their hides at the same rate as I have done, you will secure immense wealth." So they killed all their cattle, but when they offered the hides for sale they found they had been hoaxed. They were ashamed and angry at having allowed themselves to be thus imposed upon by Bitaram, and in revenge they set fire to his house at night, but he crept into a rat's hole and so escaped injury. In the morning he emerged from his hiding place, and carefully gathering up the ashes of his house tied them up in a cloth, and carried them away. As he walked along he met a merchant, to whom he said, "What have you in your bag?" He replied "Gold-pieces only." The merchant then enquired of Bitaram what he had tied up in his cloth, to which he answered, "Gold-dust only." Bitaram then said, "Will you exchange?" The merchant said, "Yes." So they exchanged, and Bitaram returned laden with gold. Not being able to count it, he again sent his wife to borrow her father's *paila*, and having measured the gold-pieces returned it to him. This time a few pieces of gold remained in the cracks in the paila, and the raja, being informed of it, went and asked Bitaram where he got the gold. He replied, "I sold the ashes of my house which you burnt over my head, and received the gold in return." The raja and his sons then enquired if the merchant, who bought the ashes from him, would buy any more. Bitaram replied, "Yes, he will buy all he can get." "Do you think," said they, "he will buy from us?" Bitaram advised them to burn their houses, and like him, turn the ashes into gold. "I had only one small house," he said, "and I obtained all this money. You have larger houses, and should therefore receive a correspondingly large amount." So they set fire to, and burnt their houses, and gathering up the ashes took them to the bazar, and there offered them for sale. After they had gone the whole length of the bazar, and had met with no buyers, some one advised them to go to where the washermen lived, saying, they might possibly take them. The washermen, however, refused, and as they could not find a purchaser, they threw away the ashes, and returned home determined to be revenged upon Bitaram.

This time they decided upon drowning him, so one day they seized him, and putting him into a bag they carried him to the river. Arrived there they put him down, and went to some little distance to cook their food. In the meantime a herd boy came up and asked Bitaram why he was tied up in the bag. He replied, "They are taking me away to marry me against my will." The herd boy said, "I will go instead of you. I wish to be married." Bitaram replied, "Open the bag and let me out, and you get in, and I will tie it up again." So Bitaram was released, and the herd boy took his place, and was afterwards thrown into the river and drowned.

Bitaram on escaping collected all the herd boy's cattle, and drove them home. When the raja and his sons returned, they found Bitaram with a large herd of cows and buffaloes. Going near, they enquired where he had got them. He replied, "At some distance below the spot where you threw me into the river, I found numerous herds of cattle, so I brought away as many as one person could drive. If you all go, you will be able to bring a very much larger number." So they said, "Very well, put us into bags, and tie us up as we did you." Bitaram replied, "It is impossible for me to carry you as you did me. Walk to the river bank, and there get into the bags, and I will push you into the river." They did as he suggested, and when all was in readiness, he pushed them into the river, and they were all drowned.

Bitaram returned alone, and took possession of all that had belonged to them. The whole kingdom became his, and he reigned peacefully as long as he lived.

1 Bita is Santali for span, and Bïtaram is span Ram, or span-long Ram.

2 A small basket with a contracted opening.

The Story of Sit and Bosont.

There was a certain raja who had two sons named Sit and Bosont. Their mother the rani had been long ill, and the raja was greatly dejected on her account. From the bed on which she lay, the rani could see two sparrows who had made their nest in a hole in the wall of the palace, and she had remarked the great love and tenderness which the hen-sparrow bore towards her young ones. One day she saw both sparrows sitting in front of their nest, and the sight of them set her a-thinking, and she came to the conclusion that the hen-sparrow was a model mother. The raja also had his attention attracted daily by the sparrows. One day, very suddenly, the hen-sparrow took ill, and died. The next day the cock-sparrow appeared with another mate, and sat in front of the nest with her, as he had done with the other. But the new mother took no notice of the young ones in the nest, but left them to die of hunger. The rani, who was greatly grieved to see such want of compassion, said to the raja, "This is how it is, one has no pity for those who belong to another. Remember what you have been a witness of, and should I die take care of the two children." Shortly after this the rani died, and the raja mourned over her, and continued most solicitous for the welfare of their two boys.

Some months after the rani's death, the raja's subjects prayed him to take another wife, saying, "Without a rani your kingdom is incomplete." The raja refused to comply, saying, "I shall never take another wife." His subjects would not, however, be silenced, but continued to press the matter upon him with such persistency that eventually he had to accede to their wishes, and take to himself another partner. He continued, however, to love and cherish his two sons Sit and Bosont.

Some time after their marriage the rani took a dislike to the elder son Sit, and was determined that he should no longer be allowed to remain within the precincts of the palace. So she feigned sickness, and the raja summoned physicians from all parts of his dominions, but without avail, as none of them could tell what the disease was from which the rani was suffering. One day when Sit and Bosont were out of the way, and the raja and she were alone together, she said to him, "Doctors and medicines will not save my life, but if you will listen to me, and do what I tell you, I shall completely recover."

The raja said, "Let me hear what it is, and I shall try what effect it may have." The rani said, "If you will promise to do for me what I shall request, I will tell you, and not otherwise." The raja replied, "I shall certainly comply with your wishes." The rani again said, "Will you without doubt, do what I wish?" The raja replied, "Yes, I shall." After she had made him promise a third time she said, "Will you take oath that you will not seek to evade fulfilling my desire?" The raja said, "I take my oath that I shall carry out your wishes to the full extent of my ability." Having thus prevailed upon the raja to pledge his word of honour, she said, "Do not allow your eldest son, Sit, to remain any longer in the palace. Order him to leave, and go somewhere else, so that I may not see his face, and never to return."

On hearing this the raja was greatly distressed. But what could he do? The rani had said, "If you permit him to remain, I shall die, and if you fulfil my wishes I shall live," and in his anxiety to save the life of his rani, he had bound himself by an oath before he knew what it was he would be required to do. After much consideration as to how he could best communicate the order to leave the palace to his son, he decided to write it on a sheet of paper and fix it, during his absence, to the door of his room. When the brothers returned, they found the paper placed there by the raja, and on reading it, were greatly troubled. After some time, during which Sit had been considering the position in which he found himself, he said to his brother, "You must remain, and I must go." On hearing his brother's words, Bosont's heart was filled with sorrow, and he replied, "Not so, I cannot see you go away alone. You have been guilty of no fault for which our parents could send you away. I cannot remain here alone. I will accompany you. We are children of the same mother, and we should not part." His brother replied, "Let us leave the house to-day. We can pass the night in some place close at hand." So they left their father's house, and concealed themselves in its vicinity. On the approach of evening they began to feel the pangs of hunger, and the younger said to the elder, "What shall we do? We have no food." After a minute's thought, the elder replied, "Although we have been sent adrift, we will take our elephants, and horses, and clothes, and money along with us." So when night had fallen, they entered the palace and brought out all that belonged to them, and at cock-crow, set forth on their journey. They travelled all day, and as the sun began to decline, they reached a dense jungle, and passing through it they came to a large city where they put up for the night. The city pleased them much, and they hired quarters in the Sarai. After they had gained a little acquaintance with their surroundings, Sit, attired in gorgeous apparel, and mounted on a splendid horse, rode every evening through the principal streets of the city. One evening the daughter of the raja of that country, from the roof of the palace, saw him ride past, and fell deeply in love with him. She immediately descended to her room, and feigning sickness, threw herself upon her couch. Her parents, on entering, found her weeping bitterly, and on enquiring the cause were informed by her attendants that she had been suddenly seized with a dangerous illness, the nature of which they did not know. The raja at once summoned the most famed physicians that could be found, to cure his daughter. One after another, however, failed to understand her complaint, and she grew worse daily. She was heard continually wailing, "I shall never recover; I shall die." After the doctors had retired baffled, she addressed her parents as follows; "You, who gave me life, listen to my entreaty. There is one expedient still, which if you will agree to put into execution, I shall recover, and be as well as formerly, and should you refuse to do as I say, and call it foolishness, then you shall never see my face again, I shall depart this life at once." On hearing these words, her parents said, "Tell us, what it is, we will surely act agreeably to your wishes." She replied, "Oh! father, promise me that you will carry them out without reserve." Her parents then promised with an oath, that they would do all she desired. Then she told her story, "Of late we have daily seen a young man in dazzling white apparel, riding and curveting his horse through the city; if you betroth me to that young prince, I shall enjoy my accustomed health again."

On hearing this, her parents became greatly distressed, as they were averse to betrothing their daughter to a stranger of whom they knew nothing. After consulting together they said, "He comes this way in the evening, let us look out for him, and see what he is like." About sunset, Sit, mounted on his horse, rode in the direction of the palace. The raja had given orders to some of his attendants to arrest the man who, every evening dressed in white, rode past the palace. So, on his appearing, they laid hold of him and led him into the presence of the raja, who being pleased with his appearance, at once introduced him to his daughter's room. She, on beholding him, instantly became well, and that same evening the two were married.

Bosont having charge of the property remained in the Sarai, while his brother went out riding. Sit not returning at his usual time, Bosont was alarmed and waited anxiously for his return. At length, being wearied, he fell asleep. During the night a gang of thieves entered his room, and began to carry off all his valuables. Bosont slept so soundly that they had time to take away everything save his bed-clothes. To obtain possession of these they had to lift him, on which he awoke and gave the alarm. The thieves beat him with their clubs till he was half dead; then, senseless and with a broken leg, they threw him into the dry bed of a river.

In the morning his servants became aware of the robbery, and also that their master was missing. His groom found him some time after in the river bed, and carried him to a doctor who bound up his limb, and took care of him. He was soon well enough to move about, but doomed to halt through life.

The raja of that country was very wealthy, and had ships on the sea. Whenever a ship left the port on its outward voyage, it was customary to carry a man on board, who, on the rising of a storm at sea, was cast over board to appease to wrath of the Spirit of the mighty Deep. Without such a victim on board, no ship could leave the harbour. Now, it so happened that one of the raja's vessels was about to sail to a foreign port, but no man suitable for the sacrifice could be obtained. At last the raja ordered them to take the lame man, whom he had seen limping about the city. He, not knowing the purpose they had in view in asking him to accompany them on their voyage, gladly embraced the opportunity of seeing foreign lands. No sooner was he on board than the ship began to move, and to obtain a better view he climbed up the mast, and sat on the top of it. In twelve days they reached a port. Bosont, however, did not decend from his elevated station, but continued gazing on the country lying around.

The daughter of the raja of that city, while walking on the roof of the palace, enjoying the cool of the evening, saw Bosont seated on the ship's mast. She at once fell violently in love with him, and descending to her room, feigned sickness. Her parents called in the most famed physicians, but their skill was of no avail, the young lady's illness increased in intensity. At last, when her parents began to give up hope of saving her life, she said, "The doctors cannot do me any good, but if you will do as I direct you, I shall recover." They said, "Tell us what it is that we can do for you." She replied, "Before I can make it known to you, you must take oath that you will not seek to evade the performance of it." To this they agreed, and the princess said, "If you will betroth me to the man sitting on the top of the mast of the vessel in the harbour, I shall immediately regain my health." The raja despatched messengers to the ship, and had Bosont brought to the palace, and solemnized their marriage that same evening.

A few days after the above occurrence, the ship was ready to set sail on her homeward voyage, so they took the lame man on board, his wife also following. After they had been a few days at sea, the vessel was in danger of foundering in a storm. The sailors searched for the victim, but he could nowhere be found. At last one of the crew looking up, spied him seated on the mast and climbing swiftly up, pushed him into the sea. His wife had brought a *tumba* with her, and seeing her husband in the sea, threw it to him. With this assistance he was able to swim to the vessel, and laying hold of the stern, followed swimming all the way to port. When the vessel was brought to anchor, he climbed up into it, and disguised himself as a fakir. The people of the city noticed him daily walking on the shore in front of the ship, and believed him to be in reality a fakir.

One day the raja seeing Bosont's wife took a fancy to her, and caused her to be brought to his palace. She had apartments assigned to her in the best part of it, and was treated with great distinction. On the raja offering her marriage, she declined, saying, "Speak not to me of it." After several days the raja enquired, "Why do you still refuse to become my wife." She replied, "Ask the fakir who is always to be seen pacing the shore in front of a vessel lying in the harbour." The raja gave orders immediately to have the fakir brought to the palace. On his being ushered into his presence, the raja said, "What do you know regarding the woman, who on declining to be my wife, referred me to you for an explanation?" In reply Bosont related in the form of a fable, the history of Sit and himself, and also what befell him after they were parted from each other. Sit, who was now raja recognized his brother in the fakir before him, and falling on his neck, wept for joy. The two brothers continued ever after to live together.

The Story of a Tiger.

A certain man had charge of a number of cattle. One day he took them to graze near a quagmire, and leaving them there went in search of jungle fruits. It so happened that one of the bullocks was browsing on the edge of the quagmire when a tiger came creeping stealthily up, and sprang upon it, but somehow or other missed his mark, and fell into the quagmire and there stuck fast. When the herd come to drive his cattle home, he found the tiger fast in the mud, and called a large number of people to come and see him. The tiger addressed those who came to gaze upon him as follows, "Oh men, pull me out. I am in great straits." They replied, "We will not pull you out even to save your life. You are a ravenous animal." The tiger said, "I will not eat you." So they pulled him out. When he was again on dry land, he said, "I will devour you, for it is my nature to do so." They replied, "Will you really eat us?" "Yes, I will," said the tiger. "Well," they rejoined, "if you will devour us, what can we do to prevent you? But let us first ask the opinion of some others as to whether it is right for you to eat us or not." So they requested the opinion of all the trees in the forest, and each said, "Human beings are all bad." On asking the Mohwa tree, it replied, "Men are not good. Behold every year I give them my flowers to eat, and my fruit from which to make oil. In the hot weather I give them shade, and on leaving, when they have rested, they give me a parting slash with their axes, therefore it is right to eat these people, as they return evil for good." So said all the trees.

From this forest they went to another in which they found a cow to whom they said, "We are come to ask your opinion on a certain matter about which we are at variance. This tiger was up to the neck in a quagmire, and we pulled him out. Now he wishes to return evil for good. Is it right for him to do so?" The cow replied, "Yes, yes, I have heard what you have got to say. You human beings are not the correct thing. Behold me, how much I have contributed to the health and comfort of my master, yet he does not recognize my merit. Now that I am old, he has turned me out, and should I improve a little in condition, he will say, 'I will take this cow to the market and sell it. I will at least get a few pence for it.' Behold, when a man is well to do, he has many friends, but when he is poor, no one knows him. Verily, you are worthy to be devoured." The tiger then said to the men, "Well, have you heard all this? Are you convinced?" They said, "Hold on, let us ask one person more." So as they walked along they saw a jackal and called to him, "Oh uncle, stand still." The jackal said, "No I cannot wait, my companions, who are on their way to see the swinging festival, are far ahead of me, and I am hurrying to overtake them." They said to him, "Wait a little and settle this matter for us. We pulled this tiger out of a quagmire, and now he wishes to devour us." The jackal then said to the tiger, "Is this true? I cannot believe that a famed individual like yourself would be fool enough to jump into a quagmire. Come, shew me the place, and how it happened." So the tiger led him to the quagmire, and said, "This is the place from which I sprang, and this is how I did it," and he leaped into the quagmire. The jackal turning to the men, said, "What are you staring at? Pelt him with stones." So they all set to and stoned the tiger to death.

Story of a Lizard, a Tiger, and a lame Man.

Once upon a time in a certain jungle, a lizard and a tiger were fighting, and a lame man, who was tending goats near by, saw them. The tiger being beaten by the lizard was ashamed to own it, and coming to the lame man said, "Tell me which of us won." The lame man being in great fear lest the tiger should eat him, said, "You won." On another occasion the lizard was compelled to flee, and took refuge in an ant hill. The tiger pursued him, but not being able to get him out, sat down to watch.

The lizard seeing his opportunity, crept stealthily up to his inveterate enemy, and climbing up his tail, fixed his teeth into his haunch, and held firmly on. The tiger felt the pain of the lizard's bite, but could not reach him to knock him off, so he ran to the lame man, and said, "Release me from this lizard." When he had caused the lizard to let go his grip, the tiger said, "Oh lame man, which of us won in the encounter?" The poor man in great fear said, "You won."

The same scene was enacted daily for many days. The tiger always came to the lame man and said, "Knock off this lizard," and after he had done so, would say, "Which of us won?" The lame man invariably replied, "You won." This had happened so often that the lame man began to feel annoyed at having to tell a lie every day to please the tiger. So one day after an ignominious flight on the part of the tiger, he being, as usual, requested to give his opinion as to who won, said, "The lizard had the best of it." On hearing this the tiger became angry, and said, "I shall eat you, my fine fellow, because you say the lizard defeated me. Tell me where you sleep." The poor lame man on hearing the tiger threaten him thus, trembled with fear, and was silent. But the tiger pressed him. He said, "Tell at once, for I shall certainly devour you." The lame man replied, "I sleep in the wall press." When night fell, the tiger set off to eat the lame man, but after searching in the wall press failed to find him. In the morning the lame man led his goats out to graze, and again met the tiger, who addressed him as follows, "You are a great cheat. I did not find you in the wall press last night." The lame man replied, "How is it you did not find me? I was sleeping there." "No," said the tiger, "you were not, you have deceived me. Now, tell me truly where you sleep." "I sleep on a rafter," said the lame man. About midnight the tiger went again in search of him to eat him, but did not find him on the rafter, so he returned home. In the morning the lame man as usual led his goats out to graze, and again encountered the tiger, who said to him, "How now! Where do you sleep? I could not find you last night." The lame man rejoined, "That is strange, I was there all the same." The tiger said, "You are a consummate liar. Now tell me plainly where you sleep at night, for I shall without doubt eat you." The lame man replied, "I sleep in the fire-place." Again the tiger went at night, but could not find him. Next morning he met the lame man, and said to him, "No more tricks, tell me where you sleep." He, thrown off his guard, said, "In the *gongo*."1

The tiger then withdrew to his den to wait till night came on, and the lame man, cursing his indiscretion, with a heavy heart, drove his goats homewards. Having made his charge safe for the night, he sat down feeling very miserable. He refused the food that was set before him, and continued bewailing his hard lot. In the hope of inducing him to eat, they gave him some mohwa wrapped in a sal leaf. This also failed to tempt him to eat; but he carried it with him when he crept into the *gongo* to sleep. At night the tiger came and lifting up the *gongo* felt it heavy, and said, "Well, are you inside?" He replied, "Yes, I am." So the tiger carried off the *gongo* with the lame man in it. By the time the tiger had gone a considerable distance, the lame man became hungry and said within himself, "I shall have to die in the end, but in the meantime I will appease my hunger." So he opened his small parcel of mohwa, and the dry leaf crackled as he did so. The noise frightened the tiger and he said, "What is it you are opening?" The lame man replied, "It is yesterday's lizard." "Hold! hold!" exclaimed the tiger, "Do not let him out yet, let me get clear away first." The lame man said, "Not so, I will not wait, but will let him out at once." The tiger being terrified at the prospect of again meeting his mortal enemy, the redoubtable lizard, threw down the *gongo* and fled, calling out, "I will not eat you. You have got the lizard with you."

In this way the lame man by means of the lizard saved his life.

1 Covering for the head and shoulders made of leaves pinned together, worn as a protection from the rain by women, while planting rice.

The Story of a Simpleton.

There was once a certain simpleton who had never seen a horse, but had heard that there was such an animal, and that men rode on his back. His curiosity was greatly excited, and he went here and there searching for a horse, so that he might ride on its back. On his way he fell in with a wag, and asked him, what horses were like, where they could be found, and whence were they produced. The wag replied, "They are very large, they are to be had at the weekly market, and they are hatched from eggs." He then asked, "What is the price of the eggs?" The other replied, "Price! They are cheap, one pice each." So one day he went to the market and bought four eggs which he saw exposed for sale, and brought them home with him. He then made preparations for a lengthened absence from his house, and started for the jungle, taking with him rice, a cooking pot and fire, to get the eggs hatched. Having reached the jungle, he placed the eggs to hatch in what turned out to be a tiger's den, and then went some distance off and sat down. After a short time he went to have a look at the eggs, and found one was missing. He was greatly distressed, at having as he fancied lost his horse, and cried out, "It has hatched, and run away somewhere. But what has happened, has happened. What can I do? I'll look out for the next one when it hatches." He then went to cook his rice, and returning after some time missed another of the eggs. He was very much grieved over the loss of the two eggs, and mourning his misfortune, cried, "Where have the two gone, after they came out of the shell? There still, however, remain two eggs." So saying, he returned to finish his cooking. After a few minutes' interval, he went to have a look at the eggs, and saw that another had disappeared; only one remained. His grief at the loss of three horses, was intense. He cried out, "Oh! where shall I find them? Three horses have been hatched, and they have all run away." He then went to where his cooking had been performed, and quickly ate his rice, and returned in all haste to look at his egg. It too was gone. On seeing this, his sorrow and disappointment were acute. He bemoaned his ill luck as follows, "After all the trouble I was at to procure my eggs, they have all hatched, and the horses are lost. But what is, must be. I shall relieve my mind by taking a chew of tobacco." After putting the tobacco into his mouth he noticed the tiger's den, and said, "It is in here, the horses have gone." So he went and broke from a tree a long stick with which he tried to poke his horses out. For some time his labours met with no reward, but at last he succeeded in forcing the tiger out of his den. Just as he was coming out, the simpleton by some chance or other got astride of his back, and called out, "At last I have found a horse." His delight was boundless. But the tiger would not go in the direction of his rider's house, but kept going further into the jungle. The simpleton then struck him about the head and ears saying, "*As ghur ghur, as ghur ghur;*"1 nevertheless the tiger plunged deeper into the jungle. At last he bolted into a thicket of trailing plants, where he unseated the simpleton. The tiger having got rid of his rider fled. Afterwards he met a jackal who said to him, "Where away, in such hot haste?" "Uh!" he said, "how much of it can I tell you! I have been greatly harassed, and distressed by *As ghur ghur*. It was with great difficulty I succeeded in giving him the slip, and now I am fleeing for dear life." The jackal said, "Come along and shew him to me, and I shall soon eat him up." The tiger replied, "Oh dear! no. I cannot go. If he finds me again he will do for me altogether." "Nonsense," said the jackal, "lead me to where he is, and I shall devour him." The tiger was persuaded, and led the way, and the jackal followed. After some little time they met a bear, who said, "Where are you two going?" The jackal gave answer, "This person has somewhere seen *As ghur ghur* and I am saying to him, 'Take me to where he is, and I shall eat him,' but he will not push ahead." Then the bear said, "Come let us all go together, and I shall eat him up." The tiger said, "I will go no further." The jackal then said, "Listen to me, I will put you upon a plan. Let us hold on by each other's tails, in this way you will have no cause to fear any evil." This suggestion pleased them well, and they cried out, "Yes, let us do that. You have hit upon a first rate expedient." Then the bear took hold of the tiger's tail, and the jackal that of the bear, and in this way they pursued their journey. But just as they drew near the thicket in which the simpleton had been left, the tiger exclaimed, "Look there, he is coming towards us," and being terribly frightened, fled at his utmost speed dragging the bear and jackal after him tearing the skin from off their bodies on the rough stones and gravel. At length the jackal cried out, "Hold on uncle, hold on uncle, you have rubbed all the skin off my body." But he would not halt, but kept dashing on through wood and brake, dragging them after him, until the bear's tail broke, and the jackal was released. His body by this time was all raw flesh, and he was swollen into a round mass. However, he managed to pick himself up, and run for his life.

Afterwards they met in with a pack of wild dogs who said, "Hulloo! what's up, that you are fleeing in such a plight?" They replied, "We are fleeing from *As ghur ghur*." "Where is he?" said they, "We will eat him." The tiger said, "There just in front of you, where you see the dark spot in the forest." So they went in the direction indicated, and while they were yet some distance off, they saw the simpleton standing in the shade of the trees. He also saw them, and being afraid hid himself in a hollow tree. On coming up to the tree in which he was, they surrounded it, and one of their number essayed to poke him out of his hiding place with his tail. The simpleton, however, taking hold of it twisted it round his hands, and pulled with all his might. The pain caused by his tail being pulled, caused the wild dog to grin. On seeing this, one of his companions said, "Oh! Brother, wherefore do you grin." He said, "I have got hold of him, and I am smiling with pleasure." The simpleton from within the tree continued to pull, till the tail of the wild dog broke, and he fell to the ground with a thud. The others on looking at him noticed that he had lost his tail. So they all became panic stricken, and fled from the place with all possible speed.

The simpleton took up his residence in that part of the jungle in which the above occurred. He is said to be the ancestor of the Bir hors, or jungle Santals.

1 Said to bullocks when ploughing to cause them to turn at the end of a furrow.

A Thief and a Tiger.

In a certain country there lived a very wealthy man whose cattle grazed on a wide plain. One day a tiger noticed them, and so did three thieves. At night the tiger came to where they were lying, and so did the three thieves, but the tiger arrived first. The night was pitch dark, and the cows getting frightened fled to their owner's premises, and all entered the cattle shed. When the tiger saw the cattle flee he ran after them, and entered the shed along with them. The thieves, coming to where they expected to find the cattle, and not seeing them, also went to the cattle shed; but the people of the house not having yet retired to rest, they hid themselves in the vicinity. When all became still, they entered the cattle shed, and began feeling for the largest and fattest oxen. Two of the thieves, each finding one to his mind, drove them away. But one man being more difficult to please than his neighbours continued to go from one to another groping for a good fat one. In this way he laid his hands on the tiger, it seemed a fat one, but lest there should be one still fatter, he left him for a little. However, as he did not find one better than the tiger he returned to him, and felt him all over again. He was without doubt the fattest in the shed, so he drove him out. On reaching the open field, the tiger went in the direction of the jungle, and his driver had great difficulty in getting him to go the road he wished. In this way,—the tiger going one direction, and the man pulling him another,—they spent the night. At cock-crow the thief became aware, that it was a tiger he had been contending with in the dark, and not an ox. He then said to the tiger, "It is you then, whom I have taken possession of." He then released the tiger, who fled to the jungle at full speed.

The thief having been awake all night felt tired, and lying down in the shade of a ridge of a rice field to rest, fell asleep.

The tiger as he ran encountered a jackal who exclaimed, "Ho! Ho! uncle, where are you off to, at such a break-neck pace?" The tiger replied, "I am going in this direction. A mite kept me awake all night, I am fleeing through fear of him." The jackal then said, "It is very strange, uncle, that you did not vanquish him. We eat such as he. Tell me where he is, and I shall soon snap him up." The tiger said, "He is over in the direction of those rice fields, asleep somewhere." The jackal then went in search of him, and soon found him asleep in the shade of a ridge of a rice field. He then went all round him reconnoitring, and when he had completed the circuit exclaimed, "The tiger said he was a mite, but he turns out to be of immense size, I cannot eat him all myself. I will gather my friends together to assist me, and then we shall devour him in no time." So he sat down with his back towards the sleeping thief, so near that his tail touched his neck, and began to yell as only a hungry jackal can. The noise awoke the sleeper, and seeing the jackal sitting so near to him, he quietly caught him by the tail, and springing on to his feet swung him round and round above his head, and then flung him from him. The jackal was severely stunned, but picking himself up, fled as fast as his legs could carry him. After he had gone some little distance he met a bear, who said, "Where away in such hot haste?" He made answer, "Uh! What can I tell you more than that that barren tiger grossly deceived me. He told me he was a mite, I went to see him and found he was a *ghur pank*,1 and without doubt he *ghur panked* me." The bear then said, "Oh! I'll eat him. Tell me where he is." The jackal said, "You will find him over in these rice fields." So the bear went to find him and eat him. When still some distance off he spied him laying asleep, and was greatly delighted, exclaiming, "My belly will be swollen with eating him before long." The thief accidentally lifted his head, and saw the bear coming straight for him, so he jumped up and ran to the nearest tree into which he climbed. The bear saw him, and went up after him, and tried to get hold of him, but he jumped from one branch to another as the bear followed him. After this had gone on for some time, it so happened that the bear missed his footing and fell heavily to the ground. The thief immediately jumped on to his back. The bear was frightened, and getting to his feet fled as fast as he could; the thief clasped him tightly round the neck, saying, "If I let go my hold he will eat me." The bear of course ran to the jungle, where the thief was caught by the branches of the trees, and dragged off his back. He did not return to the rice fields to sleep, as he feared some other animal might come to eat him, but went to his own home.

As the bear fled, he again met the jackal who asked him, "Well! did you eat him?" The bear replied, "You Sir, are a great cheat, you told me he was *ghur pank*. He is *kara upar chap*."2 The two quarrelled over the matter, and the bear tried to catch the jackal to eat him, but he managed to escape.

1 *Ghur pank* is a phrase used by ploughmen when turning their bullocks at the end of a furrow.

2 Mount the buffalo.

The Magic Fiddle

Once upon a time there lived seven brothers and a sister. The brothers were married, but their wives did not do the cooking for the family. It was done by their sister. The wives for this reason bore their sister-in-law much ill will, and at length they combined together to oust her from the office of cook and general provider, so that one of themselves might obtain it. They said, "She does not go out to the fields to work, but remains quietly at home, and yet she has not the meals ready at the proper time." They then called upon their *Bad Bonga*,1 and vowing vows unto him they secured his good will and assistance; then they said to the *Bad Bonga*, "At mid-day when our sister-in-law goes to bring water, cause it thus to happen, that on seeing her pitcher the water shall vanish, and again slowly re-appear. In this way she will be delayed. May the water not flow into her pitcher, and you keep the maiden as your own." At noon when she went to bring water, it suddenly dried up before her, and she began to weep. Then after a while the water began slowly to rise. When it reached her ankles she tried to fill her pitcher, but it would not go under the water. Being frightened she began to wail as follows;—

"Oh! my brother, the water reaches to my ankles,

Oh! my brother, the water reaches to my ankles,

Still, Oh! my brother, the pitcher will not dip,

Still, Oh! my brother, the pitcher will not dip."

The water continued to rise until it reached her knee, when she began to wail as follows;—

"Oh! my brother, the water reaches to my knee,

Oh! my brother, the water reaches to my knee,

Still, Oh! my brother, the pitcher will not dip,

Still, Oh! my brother, the pitcher will not dip."

The water continued to rise, and when it reached her waist, she wailed as follows;—

"Oh! my brother, the water reaches to my waist,

"Oh! my brother, the water reaches to my waist,

"Still, Oh! my brother, the pitcher will not dip,

"Still, Oh! my brother, the pitcher will not dip."

The water in the tank continued to rise, and when it reached her breast, she wailed as follows; —

"Oh! my brother, the water reaches to my breast,

"Oh! my brother, the water reaches to my breast,

"Still, Oh! my brother, the pitcher will not fill,

"Still, Oh! my brother, the pitcher will not fill."

The water still rose, and when it reached her neck she wailed as follows; —

"Oh! my brother, the water reaches to my neck,

"Oh! my brother, the water reaches to my neck,

"Still, Oh! my brother, the pitcher will not dip,

"Still, Oh! my brother, the pitcher will not dip."

At length the water became so deep that she felt herself to be drowning, then she wailed as follows; —

"Oh! my brother, the water measures a man's height,

"Oh! my brother, the water measures a man's height,

"Oh! my brother, the pitcher begins to fill,

"Oh! my brother, the pitcher begins to fill."

The pitcher filled with water, and along with it she sank and was drowned. The *bonga* then transformed her into a *bonga* like himself, and carried her off.

After a time she re-appeared as a bamboo growing on the embankment of the tank in which she had been drowned. When the bamboo had grown to an immense size, a *Jugi*, who was in the habit of passing that way, seeing it, said to himself, this will make a splendid fiddle. So one day he brought an axe to cut it down; but when he was about to begin, the bamboo exclaimed, "Do not cut at the root, cut higher up." When he lifted his axe to cut high up the stem, the bamboo cried out, "Do not cut near the top, cut at the root." When the *Jugi* again prepared himself to cut at the root as requested, the bamboo said, "Do not cut at the root, cut higher up;" and when he was about to cut higher up, it again called out to him, "Do not cut high up, cut at the root." The *Jugi* by this time was aware that a *bonga* was trying to frighten him, so becoming angry he cut down the bamboo at the root, and taking it away made a fiddle out of it. The instrument had a superior tone and delighted all who heard it. The *Jugi* carried it with him when he went a-begging, and through the influence of its sweet music he returned home every evening with a full wallet.

He now and again visited, when on his rounds, the house of the *bonga* girl's brothers, and the strains of the fiddle affected them greatly. Some of them were moved even to tears, for the fiddle seemed to wail as one in bitter anguish. The elder brother wished to purchase it, and offered to support the *Jugi* for a whole year, if he would consent to part with his magical instrument. The *Jugi*, however, knew its value, and refused to sell it.

It so happened that the *Jugi* sometime after went to the house of a village chief, and after playing a tune or two on his fiddle asked something to eat. They offered to buy his fiddle and promised a high price for it, but he rejected all such overtures, his fiddle being to him his means of livelihood. When they saw that he was not to be prevailed upon, they gave him food and a plentiful supply of liquor. Of the latter he partook so freely that he presently became intoxicated. While he was in this condition, they took away his fiddle, and substituted their own old one for it. When the *Jugi* recovered, he missed his instrument, and suspecting that it had been stolen requested them to return it to him. They denied having taken it, so he had to depart, leaving his fiddle behind him. The chief's son being a musician, used to play on the *Jugi's* fiddle, and in his hands the music it gave forth delighted the ears of all within hearing.

When all the household were absent at their labours in the fields, the *bonga* girl emerged from the bamboo fiddle, and prepared the family meal. Having partaken of her own share, she placed that of the chiefs son under his bed, and covering it up to keep off the dust, re-entered the fiddle. This happening every day the other members of the household were under the impression that some female neighbour of theirs was in this manner showing her interest in the young man, so they did not trouble themselves to find out how it came about. The young chief, however, was determined to watch, and see which of his lady friends was so attentive to his comfort. He said in his own mind, "I will catch her to-day, and give her a sound beating. She is causing me to be ashamed before the others." So saying, he hid himself in a corner in a pile of firewood. In a short time the girl came out of the bamboo fiddle, and began to dress her hair. Having completed her toilet, she cooked the meal of rice as usual, and having partaken herself, she placed the young man's portion under his bed, as she was wont, and was about to enter the fiddle again, when he running out from his hiding place caught her in his arms. The *bonga* girl exclaimed, "Fie! Fie! you may be a Dom,2 or you may be a Hadi."2 He said, "No. But from to-day, you and I are one." So they began lovingly to hold converse with each other. When the others returned home in the evening, they saw that she was both a human being and a *bonga*, and they rejoiced exceedingly.

Through course of time the *bonga* girl's family became very poor, and her brothers on one occasion came to the chief's house on a visit.

The *bonga* girl recognised them at once, but they did not know who she was. She brought them water on their arrival, and afterwards set cooked rice before them. Then sitting down near them, she began in wailing tones to upbraid them on account of the treatment she had been subjected to by their wives. She related all that had befallen her, and wound up by saying, "It is probable that you knew it all, and yet you did not interfere to save me."

After a time she became reconciled to her sisters-in-law, and no longer harboured enmity in her mind against them, for the injury they had done her.

1 The spirit believed to preside over a certain class of rice land.

2 Semi-Hinduised aborigines, whose touch is considered polluting.

Gumda, the Hero.

There was once a certain fatherless lad named Gumda. His occupation was to tend the raja's goats. He, and his mother lived in a small house at the end of the street in which the raja's palace was situated. The raja's mahout was in the habit of taking his elephant along that street, and every time it passed, it rubbed itself against the wall of Gumda's house. One day at noon it so happened that Gumda was at home when the elephant was being taken to the tank to drink, and as usual he rubbed his side against the house as he passed. Gumda was incensed with the elephant for thus destroying his house, and coming out quickly, said to the mahout, "What although it is the raja's elephant! I could take hold of any person's elephant by the trunk, and throw it across seven seas." The elephant understood what Gumda had said, and he refused to go down into the water, and would not even drink. On being brought home he would not eat his grain, nor would he so much as look at water. He continued thus so long that he began to grow lean and weak. The mahout knew that it was Gumda's curse that had so affected his charge. The raja one day noticing the altered condition of his elephant, said to the mahout, "Why has the elephant become so emaciated?" The mahout replied, "Oh! raja, one day at noon Gumda abused him. He said, 'If you were not the raja's elephant, I would take you by the trunk and throw you across seven seas.' 'Every day,' he said, 'he rubs himself against my house.' Since then the elephant has refused his food and water." The raja, on hearing this, commanded that Gumda be brought before him. The messenger found him at home, and brought him into the presence of the raja who asked him, "Is it true, Gumda, that you said you would throw the elephant as you would a stone?" Gumda replied, "Yes, it is quite true that I said so. The elephant every time it passes along the street rubs itself against the wall of my house, and being angry, I said these words. Now, do with me whatsoever you please." The raja marvelled greatly on hearing Gumda's reply, and addressing him said, "Now my lad, prove your words, for prove them you must. If you succeed in thus throwing an elephant, I shall present you with a large estate." The raja appointed the tenth day following as that on which Gumda should wrestle with the elephant; and he, after receiving permission from the raja, returned home.

The raja in the interval caused proclamation to be made to all his subjects, ordering them to be present on the day when Gumda was to meet the elephant in mortal combat. On the morning of the appointed day Gumda was found baking bread. As he did not appear punctually in the arena, the raja sent a messenger to bring him. On arriving at Gumda's house, he found him baking bread. He said to him, "Come along, the raja has asked for you." Gumda said, "Wait a little till I partake of some refreshment." He invited the messenger to be seated, and he also sat down as if to eat, but instead of eating the bread, he began to throw it at the man, and continued doing so until he had buried him under eight maunds of loaves. The poor fellow cried out, "Oh Gumda, come and release me, of a truth I am almost crushed to death under this heap of bread." He removed the bread from above him, and he immediately returned to the raja. As he was leaving the house he saw 12 maunds of cooked rice, evidently intended for Gumda's dinner. Coming into the presence of the raja he said, "Oh! raja, I saw in Gumda's house twelve maunds of cooked rice, and he threw a loaf of bread weighing eight maunds at me, which almost crushed me to death. It is quite possible that he may win."

At length Gumda came bringing with him a sledge hammer weighing twelve maunds, and a shield of the same weight. The contest was to take place on a plain sufficiently large to accommodate an immense number of spectators.

Then the fight began. The two combatants attacked each other so furiously that they raised such a cloud of dust as to completely conceal them from the onlookers. The elephant could not long sustain the unequal combat, and when he was beaten, Gumda seized him by the trunk, and threw him over the seas. Owing to the darkness caused by the clouds of dust, none of the thousands present noticed the elephant as he went, flying over their heads high up in the air.

When the dust subsided, Gumda was found sitting alone, the elephant was nowhere to be seen. The raja called the victor to him, and said, "What have you done with the elephant?" Gumda replied "I flung him early in the forenoon over seven seas." Hearing his answer and not seeing the elephant, they all marvelled greatly.

The raja then said to Gumda, "Well, you have thrown the elephant somewhere. You must now go in search of its bones." Gumda went home and said to his mother, "Make up a parcel of food for me, I am going to find the elephant's bones." She complied with his request and he set out.

As he hurried along intent upon his quest, he found a man fishing with a Palmyra palm tree as a rod, and a full grown elephant as a bait. On seeing him

Gumda exclaimed, "You are indeed a great hero." The man replied, "I am no hero, the widow's son Gumda is the great hero, for did not he fling the raja's elephant across seven seas?" Gumda said, "I am he." The fisherman said," I will go with you." Gumda replied, "Come along!"

As Gumda and his attendant went on their way, they came to a field in which a number of men were hoeing, and their master, to shield them from the heat of the sun, stood holding over them, as an umbrella, a large Pepul tree.1 Gumda seeing him]said, "You are a hero and no mistake." The man replied, "No indeed, I am no hero. Gumda, the widow's son, threw the raja's elephant across seven seas. He is the hero." Gumda said, "I am he." "Then," said the man, "I also will go with you." "Follow me," said Gumda, and the three proceeded on their way.

As they journeyed they fell in with two men, who were raising water from a tank for irrigating purposes by merely singing. When Gumda saw them, he exclaimed, "You two are heroes indeed." They answered, "What do you see heroic in us? There is one hero, Gumda by name, he threw a raja's elephant across seven seas." Gumda said, "I am he." The men exclaimed, "We also will follow you." Gumda said, "Follow." And the five men went forth to search for the elephant's bones.

On and on they went until they reached the sea, which they crossed, and entered the primeval forest beyond. Selecting a suitable place they encamped, and began the search for the elephant's bones. The first day the fisherman was left in the camp to cook the food, while the others went out into the forest. Near by a certain *jugi* raja resided in a cave in a rock. He came to the camp just as the food was cooked, and said to the fisherman, "Give me some rice to eat." He declined, and the *jugi* raja then said, "Will you give me rice, or will you fight with me?" He replied, "I have prepared this food with difficulty and prefer fighting to giving it up." So they fought, and the *jugi* raja was victor. He laid a heavy stone on the breast of the cook, and then devoured all the food. There had been twelve maunds of rice prepared, and he left none. After a long time he released his victim, and then went his way. Being released the fisherman set about preparing more food, but before it was ready, his companions returned and seeing the pot still on the fire, they enquired why he had not made haste with his cooking. He replied, "I have not been idle, I have spent all the time in cooking." He did not tell them about the *jugi* raja having been at the camp.

The next day another of the company remained as cook, while the others went out to search in the forest for the elephant's bones. The *jugi* raja again visited the camp, and the scene of the previous day was re-enacted. But he also did not speak of the visit of the *jugi* raja to the others when they returned.

In this way the *jugi* raja encountered each in turn till only Gumda was left, and he remained in the camp to cook. When he had got the rice cooked, the *jugi* raja made his appearance and said, "Will you fight with me, or will you give up the food?" Gumda replied, "I will not give you the food. I have spent much time in cooking it, and when those who have gone in search of the elephant's bones return, what shall I set before them, if I give it to you now? You have played this trick every day, and have put my companions to much trouble, but to-day we have met." So they fought. Gumda overpowered the *jugi* raja, and killed him with the stone he used to put upon the breast of those whom he vanquished. He then espoused the *jugi* raja's wife, and took possession of his kingdom. Gumda's companions held him in great awe, because each in turn had been conquered by the *jugi* raja, but Gumda had experienced little difficulty in putting him to death.

Gumda became raja of that country, and when he had settled his affairs, he sent for his mother to come and reside with him. The raja, whom Gumda had previously served, sought his friendship, and withdrew his command to Gumda to search for the elephant's bones until he found them. The prowess of Gumda caused him to deprecate his anger. He said, "If I offend him, he will kill me as he did the *jugi* raja, and take my wife and kingdom, as he did his."

1 Ficus religiosa, Willd. one of the hugest of India's many huge trees.

Lipi, and Lapra.

Once upon a time there were seven brothers. At first they were very poor, but afterwards they became comparatively rich, and were in position to lay out a little money at usury. The affairs of the youngest prospered most, so that before long he became the wealthiest of them all.

Each of the seven brothers planted fruit trees, and every day after they returned from their work, before they sat down to meat, they watered them. In process of time all the trees flowered, but the flowers on the eldest brother's trees withered and dropped off the day they appeared. The trees of the other brothers failed to ripen their fruit, but those of the youngest brother were laden with delicious fruit which ripened to perfection. Five of the brothers said to him, "You are very fortunate in having such a splendid crop;" but the eldest brother was envious of his good fortune, and resolved to be revenged upon him.

The youngest brother brought up two puppies, whom he named Lipi and Lapra. They turned out good hunting dogs, and by their aid their master used to keep the family larder well supplied. The others were pleased to see so much game brought to the house. One day they said to him, "Take us also to where you get your large game." To this he agreed, and they accompanied him to his usual hunting ground. Game was plentiful, but they could kill nothing, although every time he shot an arrow he brought down his animal. Five of his brothers praised him for his skill, and accuracy of aim, but the eldest brother, not having succeeded in bagging anything himself, envied him still more, and was confirmed in his desire for revenge.

It so happened that one day all the brothers, with the exception of the eldest and the youngest, went out to their work. The eldest brother finding himself alone with his youngest brother proposed that they should go together to the hill for the purpose of procuring fibre to make ropes. He said, "Come let us go to the hill to cut *lar*."1 His brother replied, "Come, let us set out." He, however, wished to take his dogs with him, but his brother said, "Why should you tire them by taking them so far? Leave them behind." But he replied, "I shall not go, unless you allow me to take them with me. How shall we be able to bring home venison if they do not accompany us? They may kill some game on the way." As he insisted, he was permitted to do as he desired, and they set out for the hill.

As they went on their way they came to a spring, and the elder said, "Tie up the two dogs here. I know all this forest, and there is no game to be found in it." The younger was averse to leaving his dogs behind him, but as his brother seemed determined he should do so, he tied them with a stout rope to a tree. His brother said, "See that you make them secure, so that they may not break loose and run away, and be lost."

A low hill lay between them, and the high one on which the trees grew which yielded the *lar*. This they surmounted, and descending into the valley that divided them began the ascent, and soon reached the place where their work was to be. They soon cut and peeled sufficient *lar*, and sitting down twisted it into strong ropes. Just as they had prepared to return home, the elder brother seized the younger, and bound him with the ropes they had made. He then grasped his sickle with the intention of putting him to death. The helpless young man thought of his dogs, and in a loud voice wailed as follows; —

Come, come, Lipi and Lapra,

Cross the low hill

On to the slope of the high.

He called them again and again. The dogs heard the voice, and struggled to get loose, and at length, by a great effort, they succeeded in breaking the ropes with which they were bound, and ran in the direction from which the sound proceeded. Now and again the cries ceased, and they stood still until they again heard them, when they ran as before. Having reached the valley that separated the two hills, they could no longer hear the wailing as before, and they were greatly perplexed. They ran hither and thither, hoping to catch it again, but not doing so they directed their course to the large hill, on reaching the foot of which it again became audible. They now recognized the voice of their master, and ran rapidly forward.

When the elder brother saw the dogs approaching, he quickly aimed a blow with the sickle at his younger brother's head, but he, jerking aside, escaped. Before there was time for him to strike again, the dogs had arrived, and their master hounded them upon his assailant and they quickly tore him to pieces. They then bit through the ropes with which his brother had bound him, and set him at liberty. He then returned home accompanied by his dogs, and when they enquired of him where his brother was, he replied, "He left me to follow a deer, I cannot say what direction he took. We did not meet again." He wept as he related this, and they enquired, "Why do you weep?" He said,

"My two dogs lay down on the ground, and howled, and fear possesses me that some wild beast has devoured my brother."

The next day a party went in search of him, and found him as the dogs had left him. When they saw him lying torn and bloody, they said, "Some wild beast has done this."

They brought the body home, and committed it to the flames of the funeral pile, and sorrowfully performed all the ceremonies usual on such occasions.

After the death of the elder brother, they all lived together in peace and harmony.

1 The fibre yielded by Bauhinia Vahlii, W. and A. goes under that name among the Santals.

The Story of Lelha.

I.

There once lived a certain raja, who had three wives. The two elder had two sons each, and the younger only one, whose name was Lelha.1 The four sons of the first two wives were very friendly with each other, being seldom separate, but they despised Lelha, and never permitted him to join them in any of their pastimes or sports.

The raja had a plot of ground set apart for a flower garden, but there was nothing in it. One day a certain *Jugi* came to him, and said, "Oh! raja, if you fill your garden with all kinds of flowering plants, your whole city will appear enchanting." Having said this, the *Jugi* went to his home. The raja was greatly affected by what the *Jugi* had said, and was immediately seized with a fit of the sulks. There was an apartment in the palace set apart for the exclusive use of those who happened to be in that state of mind. Such an one shut himself up in this chamber until the fit wore off, or until he was persuaded to be himself again.

The raja refused his evening meal, and as was his wont, when in this frame of mind, retired to the sulking apartment, and lay down. The two elder ranis having been informed of what had occurred, hasted to the raja, and said, "Oh! raja, why are you sulking?" He replied, "This morning a *Jugi* came to me and said, that if I planted flowering shrubs in my garden the whole city would appear enchanting. If any one will do this work for me, I will rise, if not, I shall remain here." The ranis then addressed him thus, "Oh! raja, rise up, and eat and drink." The raja replied, "Let the young men come to me, I will do as you desire." The two ranis then left, and calling their sons, sent them to their father. Coming into the presence of the raja they said, "Wherefore father are you sulking?" The raja replied, "If you plant flowers in my flower garden I shall be comforted, and shall leave my couch." They said, "Is it on this account you are distressed? We shall cause the garden to be filled with flowers in a short time." On receiving this assurance the raja left his bed, and partook of food, and was refreshed. Lelha's mother now appeared on the scene, and addressing the raja, said, "Wherefore, raja are you sulky?" He replied, "Who told you I was sulky?" She replied, "A shopkeeper gave me the

58 | Santal Folk Tales

information." Then the raja got angry, and ordered her to leave, but she said, "If you do not tell me why you are sulking I will not depart, am not I also your humble maidservant? Unless you tell me, I will not go, I will die here rather than leave." The raja relented, and related to her all the words of the *Jugi*. She then returned home.

Her son Lelha entered the house soon after her arrival. He had been engaged in some field sports, and being wearied and hungry, said to his mother, "Give me some cooked rice." She was annoyed with him and said, "Although the raja is ill, your first cry is for boiled rice." Lelha on hearing this went to his father, and enquired what was wrong. But the raja flying into a rage scolded him, saying, "Go away Lelha. What do you want here? Never come near me again. Did not I build a house for your mother and you at the extreme end of the street, away from here? Be off, or I shall beat you." To which Lelha replied, "Oh! father raja, am not I also a son of yours? Let me be foolish or otherwise, still, I am your son, and unless you inform me of what has grieved you, I shall die rather than leave this." Then the raja told him also. He said, "It is because I do not see flowers in the garden." "Oh!" said Lelha, "Is that what distresses you?" He then left.

The raja's four elder sons caused all manner of flowering shrubs and trees to be planted in the garden, and in a short time it was in a blaze of colour, so much so, that the whole city was as if lighted thereby.

Just at this time, when every tree, shrub and plant was covered with blossom another *Jugi*, named Koema *Jugi*, came to the city and said to one and another, "You, the citizens of this city, are covering yourselves with renown, but if you attach *hiras* 2 and *manis* 3 to the branches, you will add renown to renown." The *Jugi's* words reached the raja, and he was so much affected by them, that he immediately began to sulk, and on being questioned by his two ranis, he replied, "Do you not remember the words of the Koema *Jugi*?" They said, "Yes, we remember. He said, 'if you place *hiras* and *manis* in this garden the whole country will be resplendent'." "On that account then, I am sulking, and if I do not see *hiras* and *manis*, I shall not partake of any food." At the raja's words the two ranis returned sorrowfully to their apartments.

At that moment their four sons entered the house and asked for food. The ranis were annoyed, and said, "The raja, your father, is sulking, and you must have food and drink." On learning their father's state the youths were distressed on his account, and went to him weeping, and enquired why he was sulking. He related to them the words of Koema *Jugi*, and added, "Unless I see *hiras* and *manis* attached to the branches of the trees in my flower garden, I shall not rise from my couch." His four sons replied, "Is it for this reason you are grieving? We will search for, and bring them, and if we fail, then sulk again, and refuse your food, and die of hunger, and we will not prevent you, only listen to us this time and get up." The raja was persuaded to rise, and having partaken of food he was refreshed.

II.

The raja had planted flowering shrubs in his garden, but the *Indarpuri Sadoms* 4 ate up all the flowers as they appeared, and so he again began to sulk. He said, "I planted bushes, but I see no flowers. What reason is there for my remaining alive?" And going to the sulking chamber he lay down, and as usual refused to eat. Then there was confusion in the household, and running hither and thither. The two ranis went to him, but he was annoyed, and ordered them to leave, saying, "I will not rise, by your telling me," so they returned weeping, each to her own apartment.

Just then their four sons returned from hunting, and demanded food. Their mothers were annoyed, and said, "You young gentlemen are hungry, and must have food, that the raja is sulking is nothing to you, if you are fasting." On hearing this the sons went to their father, and enquired, "Oh! father, wherefore are you sulking?" The raja replied, "Oh! my sons, I am sulking because I see no flowers in my garden. Unless I see flowers in my garden, I shall not remain in this world." His sons replied, "Give us three days, and if at the end of that time you see no flowers, then you may sulk." He was persuaded to rise, and having bathed, and partaken of food, he was refreshed.

Just then Lelha arrived, and addressing the raja said, "Oh! raja, what ails you?" The raja on seeing Lelha was angry, and scolded him severely. He said, "Has Lelha come here? Drive him away at once." Lelha left without uttering another word.

After three days the raja began again to sulk, because there were still no flowers to be seen in his garden. The *Indarpuri Sadoms* came about mid-night and ate up all the buds. The raja's four elder sons when watching could not remain awake for one hour, and so the *Indarpuri Sadoms* came nightly and devoured all the buds that should have burst into flower in the morning, so that not one solitary blossom was to be seen. For this reason the raja again began to sulk, and no one dared to say anything to him.

At this juncture Lelha's mother went from her own house to a shop to buy rice. The shopkeeper refused to supply her. He said, "The raja is sulking, and she comes here to buy rice. I will not weigh it, so go." Lelha's mother went hastily home, and encountered Lelha returning from a stroll. Lelha asked for food. He said, "Oh! mother, give me cooked rice quickly." She rebuked him, and said, "The raja is sulking. The shopkeeper refused to give me rice, how can I give you food? I am a prey to grief, and here my young gentleman is hungry. Go to the raja."

Lelha did as his mother ordered him, and went to the apartment where the raja was, and called several times, "Oh! father, get up." At length the raja asked, "Who are you? Do not irritate me. Go away at once." Lelha replied, "I am your humble slave and son, Lelha." His father said, "Wherefore have you come here? Lelha, Go home, or else I shall beat you. What do you want here? If you go, go at once, if not, I shall have you chastised." Lelha replied, "Because you, Oh! raja, are sulking. The shopkeeper in the bazaar refused to sell to my mother rice, saying, 'something is amiss with the raja, I cannot let you have it.'" The raja then said, "Go, and bring the shopkeeper here." To which Lelha replied, "Why are you sulking? If you do not tell me, it were better for me to die here. I cannot leave you. I have come here fasting, not having eaten anything to-day." The raja said, "Your four brothers have not been able to do anything, and what can I hope from telling you about it, Lelha?" Lelha replied, "It is still possible that I may accomplish something, but although I should not, yet I am a son of yours. Do tell me. If you die, I shall die also. We will depart this life together. I cannot return home." The raja then thought within himself, I will tell him, and let him go. If I do not do so, Lelha may die along with me. Then addressing Lelha, he said, "It is nothing child, only I see no flowers in my garden, and therefore I am sulking. Although your four brothers watched three nights, still I see no flowers." Lelha then said, "If my brothers watched three nights, see me watch one." The raja replied, "Very good my son, let us leave this apartment."

The raja went to bathe, and Lelha going to the shopkeeper bought several kinds of grain, which he carried home and gave to his mother, saying, "Roast a seer of each, and cook some rice for me. I have succeeded in persuading my father to rise. He has bathed and dined, and is refreshed. He was sulking because he can see no flowers in his garden. It was with great difficulty that I prevailed upon him to get up." His mother said, "What does my Lord want with roasted grain?" Lelha replied, "Let me do with it as I chose, you prepare it. I will take it with me at night when I go to watch in the flower garden." His mother said, "Have you forgotten your brothers' threats to beat you?" Lelha replied, "My brothers may beat me, but no other person. What help is there for it?"

At nightfall, Lelha, having supped, tied up in the four corners of his plaid four kinds of roasted grain, and entering the garden climbed up on a raised platform, and began his vigil.

After a short time he untied one of his parcels of roasted grain, and began leisurely to eat it, one grain at a time. Just as he had consumed the last one, an *Indarpuri Sadom* descended from the East and alighted in the garden to browse upon the flowers. Lelha seeing it, crept noiselessly up, and laid hold of it, and at the same instant its rider, an *Indarpuri Kuri*,5 exclaimed, "Hands off! Lelha. Hands off! Lelha. Touch me not." Lelha replied, to the *Indarpuri Kuri*, "Besides touching you, I will bind and detain you till morning. You have become bold. You have caused my father to fast; but I have captured you to-night. Where will you go?" "Let me go," she said, "I will bless you." Lelha rejoined, "You are deceiving me." The *Indarpuri Kuri* made answer, "I am not deceiving you. I shall give you whatever blessing you may desire. Place your hand upon my head, Lelha." He did so, and a lock of hair adhered to his hand, when he withdrew it. The *Indarpuri Kuri* then said, "When you desire anything, take that lock of hair into your hand, and say, Oh! *Indarpuri Kuri*, give me this or that, and instantly you shall receive it. Of a truth it shall be so. I shall never fail you." Lelha then released the *Indarpuri Sadom*, and it mounted up into the air, and he and his *Indarpuri* Rider vanished into space.

By the time Lelha had eaten all the roasted grain from another corner of his plaid, another *Indarpuri Sadom* with his *Indarpuri Kuri* rider descended from the West. Lelha caught these as he had done the first. This Kuri was a younger sister of the other, and she gave a like blessing to Lelha before he released her horse.

Lelha now began to eat his third parcel of roasted grain, and just as he had finished it he saw another *Indarpuri Sadom* with an *Indarpuri Kuri* rider descend from the North, and alight in the garden. Lelha also captured these. The rider was a younger sister of the last. She also gave Lelha a blessing, and was allowed to go.

At cockcrow, Lelha, having eaten the last grain of his fourth parcel, looked up and beheld an *Indarpuri Sadom* with an *Indarpuri Kuri* rider descend into the garden from the North. She was the youngest of the sisters. Lelha crept stealthily up, and laid hold of the horse's mane. The *Indarpuri Kuri* then exclaimed, "Hands off! Lelha. Hands off! Lelha." Then Lelha replied, "You Lelha greatly this morning. It is almost dawn, where can you go to escape punishment?" Then the *Indarpuri Kuri* said, "Oh! Lelha, We are four sisters, daughters of one mother, I will give you a blessing." Lelha replied, "In this way three persons have fled. You also appear the same." The *Indarpuri Kuri* said, "We four sisters have one blessing. Place your hand upon my head, and release me." Lelha did so, and the *Indarpuri Sadom* on being liberated sailed off into the sky with his *Indarpuri* rider. Lelha tied the four locks of hair of the *Indarpuri Kuris* each in a corner of his plaid, as he had before done with the roasted grain. When the day fully dawned he returned to his home weeping, for his four brothers seeing the bushes laden with blossom were envious of him, and had hurled him headlong to the ground from off the raised platform on which he sat.

On reaching home his mother said to him, "You see your brothers have beaten you. I warned you against going." Lelha replied, "What help is there for it? My brothers beat me. No one else did. I must bear it." His mother said, "Then, why do you let others know?"

In the morning the raja said, "Last night Lelha was watching. I will go and take a look at the garden." He went and found a perfect sea of blossom, the sight of which almost overcame him.

It so happened that as the raja gazed upon the fairy scene around him, Koema *Jugi* turned up, and addressing the raja said, "You are lost in wonder, but if you hang *hiras* and *manis* on the branches the whole country will be resplendent. Then your wonder and amazement will be increased twentyfold."

III.

The raja's garden was without an equal in the world, but the words of Koema *Jugi* had caused him to become discontented with it, and because there were neither *hiras* nor *manis* hanging from the branches he, as before, began to sulk. They reasoned with him saying, "Do not grieve over it. We will bring *hiras* and *manis*." So he rose, and having bathed partook of some refreshment.

About this time Lelha's mother went to a shop to purchase food. On seeing her the shopkeeper said, "Something is amiss with the raja, and she is hungry, and comes here giving annoyance. Go away. I will not weigh anything for you." So she returned home empty-handed. As she entered the house she encountered Lelha just returned from hunting, who said, "Oh! mother, give me cooked rice." His mother replied, "Something is wrong with the raja, and here my young lord is fasting, and cries for food. He is greatly concerned about his own affairs."

Lelha went at once to the raja, and enquired "What ails you, father?" The raja replied, "Is there anything ailing me? Has Lelha come here? I will beat him shortly." Lelha said, "Do with me what you please. Why are you sulking? If you do not tell me, although it should cost me my life, I will not leave, rather slay me here at once." The raja thought within himself, "He annoys me, I will tell him to get rid of him." So he said, "Your brothers have gone in search of *hiras* and *manis*, and it is because I do not see the trees in my garden adorned with these precious stones that I am sulking. Lelha said, "I will also go." His father said, "Do not go child." But Lelha was determined, and disregarded his father's command.

Lelha went to the bazaar and purchased rice and *dal*, and his mother when she saw him bringing them home with him, said, "What is wrong? You are completely out of breath." Lelha replied, "My brothers have gone to search for *hiras* and *manis*, and I also am busy preparing to follow them." She tried to dissuade him saying, "Although the mean fellows beat you, still you will not keep away from them." Lelha quickly replied, "What help is there for it, mother? Let my brothers beat me or not, what is that to me? I must bear it all." So his mother prepared food, and Lelha, having partaken of it, set out.

He went to the stable, and saddled the lame horse, as his brothers had taken away the good ones, and mounting rode to the outskirts of the city. He then dismounted, and turned the lame horse loose, and went into the raja's flower garden, and said, "Oh! *Indarpuri Kuri*, give me a horse instantly. My brothers have left me behind, and gone I know not where. Give me such a horse as will enable me to reach them at once." Immediately a horse was at his side, and in a few seconds he was in sight of his brothers. He then alighted from his horse, and said "Oh! *Indarpuri Kuri*, I return your horse," and instantly it disappeared, and he overtook his brothers on foot.

When his brothers saw him, they said, "He has overtaken us." Some of them said, "Catch him and beat him," others said, "No, let him alone, he will do our cooking. We can go in search of *hiras* and *manis*, and leave him to guard our camp. Come let us push on, we have now got a good guard for our camp." This pleased all, and they said, "It is now evening, let us pitch our camp for the night." They did so, and Lelha soon had supper ready, of which having partaken they all retired to rest.

In the morning Lelha again acted as cook, and while it was yet early set breakfast before his brothers, and they having eaten, mounted their horses, and went in search of *hiras* and *manis*. They were now a month's journey distant from their own home, and the raja of the country in which they were, had just opened a new bazaar. It was a large and beautiful bazaar, and an *Indarpuri Kuri* had a stall it. This *Indarpuri Kuri* had given out, that whoever would go and come twelve kos seven times within an hour should be her husband.

The four sons of the raja, who had come in search of *hiras* and *manis* hearing this said, "Some one from amongst us four brothers must marry this girl. Let us exercise our horses, it is possible that some one of them may do the distance in the specified time." They had left home in search of *hiras* and *manis*, and now were scheming to secure the *Indarpuri Kuri* as the wife of one of them. So they returned to camp, and sitting down began to discuss the subject. They said, "If our horses are well exercised, no doubt, but that they will be able to run the distance in the time. Therefore, let us diligently train our horses, so that they may be able to accomplish the task."

While they were thus engaged, Lelha said, "What is it, brothers, that you are discussing?" His brothers rebuked him, saying, "Why are you eavesdropping? We will beat you." They did not, however, beat him, as they feared he would return home, and leave them without a cook. So he cooked the supper and set it before them, and when they had eaten, they retired to rest.

In the morning Lelha again prepared the food, and his four brothers having breakfasted, mounted and rode off to the bazaar, and there exercised their horses. After they had left Lelha collected all the brass vessels, and what other property there was, and carefully hid them away. Then he called to the *Indarpuri Kuri*, "Oh! *Indarpuri Kuri*, give me a horse," and instantly, just such a horse as he desired stood beside him. He mounted and galloping away soon overtook his brothers. He saluted them, but they did not recognize him. He said to them, "Wherefore, brothers, have you brought your horses to a standstill? Make them race." They replied, "We were waiting for you. We are tired. It is your turn now." Lelha immediately switched up his horse, and away it flew at such a pace, that it could scarcely be seen. That day his horse ran twelve kos there and back three times within an hour. At the end of the race soldiers tried to lay hold of Lelha's horse, but he called out, "Do not touch him. He will not allow you to lay a finger on me." The soldiers said, "The raja has given orders, that the horse that ran three, or five, or seven times is to be brought before him." Lelha replied, "Go, and tell the raja, that the horse bites, so we could not stop him. The raja will not be displeased with you." He then rode away to the camp, and having returned the horse to the *Indarpuri Kuri* he began to prepare the evening meal, which was ready by the time his four brothers arrived.

After supper they began to talk over the events of the day, wondering who owned the horse that had run so well. Lelha drew near, and said, "What is it, brothers, that you are talking about?" Some said, "Beat him, what has he got to do listening?" Others said, "Do not beat him, he cooks for us." So the matter ended, and all lay down for the night.

In the morning Lelha again prepared the food, and his brothers having breakfasted, mounted their horses, and rode off to the bazaar, where they raced as usual. After they had gone, Lelha gathered all their property together, and hid it as he had done on the day previous. Then, mounting an *Indarpuri Sadom*, he followed his brothers, and on coming up with them saluted them, but they did not recognize him as their brother. Then a conversation similar to that of the previous day passed between Lelha and his brothers. This time Lelha's horse ran the distance, there and back, five times within the hour. The raja's soldiers again attempted to stop Lelha's horse, but he told them that it was in the habit of biting, so they allowed him to pass, and he galloped off to the camp, and returning the horse to the *Indarpuri Kuri* began to prepare the evening meal. When his brothers arrived Lelha set food before them, and they ate and drank. After they had supped they sat and talked about the wonderful horse, and its feat that day. Lelha again enquired what they were talking about, but they rebuked him saying, "Do not listen. It is not necessary for you to know what we are speaking about." They all then retired for the night.

Early next morning Lelha set about preparing breakfast, and his brothers, having partaken of it, set out for the bazaar. After their departure Lelha gathered everything together, and hid them as before, and then called upon *Indarpuri Kuri* for a horse. The horse came, and Lelha mounted and galloped after his brothers. On overtaking them he saluted, and then said, "Wherefore, brothers, do you stand still? Race your horses." They replied, "It is your turn now. We have run, and our horses are tired." Lelha then started his horse, and it ran twelve kos there, and twelve kos back, seven times within the hour. The raja's soldiers again attempted to capture Lelha's horse, but he prevented them, and so returned to the camp. When he had returned the horse to the *Indarpuri Kuri* he resumed his office of cook, and had supper ready by the time his brothers returned. They sat down together, and began to discuss the wonderful performance of the horse which had that day done the distance seven times in one hour. Lelha again enquired, "What is it that you are talking about, brothers?" Some one said, "Beat him. He has no right to be listening," but another said, "Do not beat him, he cooks our food." When the four brothers were tired talking Lelha set supper before them, and having supped, they lay down to sleep.

Next morning Lelha cooked the breakfast as usual, and his brothers having partaken of it, mounted their horses, and rode off to the bazaar. After they had left Lelha put everything]out of sight, as usual. Then he desired the *Indarpuri Kuri* to give him a horse, and having mounted, he followed his brothers, and on coming near saluted them as before, but again they failed to recognize him.

IV.

On the seventh day Lelha again followed his brothers to the bazaar. He begged the *Indarpuri Kuri* to give him a horse that would do the distance there and back seven times within the hour, and at the end would fall down dead, and also to have another horse ready for him to mount. The *Indarpuri Kuri* gave him his desire and he rode off to the bazaar, and again saluted his brothers, and at the same time pushed his horse close up to them. They called out, "Keep your horse back, he will crush us." Lelha then enquired why they were standing still. They replied, "We were waiting for you." So Lelha put his horse to the gallop, and did the distance there and back seven times within an hour. On his return the last time the soldiers attempted to lay hold of the horse, but Lelha said, "Let him alone, I will go myself." At the same instant his horse fell, and he leapt from it, and having returned it to the *Indarpuri Kuri*, he mounted the other, and rode from the race course to the bazaar, and was united in wedlock to the *Indarpuri Kuri*.

After the marriage he informed his bride that he was in search of *hiras* and *manis* for his father's flower garden. She informed him, that lying on the breast of her elder sister, who had been sleeping for twelve years, was a large quantity of *hiras*. "To obtain them you must first," she said, "buy two bundles of grass, two goats, and a pair of shoes, and make two ropes each two hundred cubits long. My sister is guarded by an elephant, a tiger, and a dog. On entering you will first encounter the elephant, and you must throw him a bundle of grass. A little farther on you will meet the tiger, you must give him a goat. Then you will see the dog, and you must throw him a shoe. When you are returning you must do the same. Throw a shoe to the dog, a goat to the tiger, and a sheaf of grass to the elephant. You must lose no time in possessing yourself of the *hiras* you will find on my sister's breast. If you delay, her army may take you prisoner." She also said, "My sister's house is situated on an island in a large lake, and you can only reach it by hiring a boat. The door of her house is a large heavy stone, which you must remove before gaining an entrance. On the island there is a Sinjo tree,6 with branches on the North side, and on the South. On the branches of the South side there are the young of *hiras* and *manis*, but on those of the North side there is nothing. On the South side there are five branches, and within the fruit there are *manis*. Do not forget this. The large *hira*, which glitters on my sister's breast, is the mother *hira*." Just as she concluded the foregoing instructions the cock crew, and she added, "See that you remember all I have told you."

Then Lelha left his bride to return to his brothers. As he went he remembered that they would be sure to abuse him for having been absent, so he collected a large number of shells, and stringing them together, hung them round his neck, and went dancing to the camp. When his brothers saw him, in the dress of a merryandrew they rebuked him severely.

V.

Lelha's excuse for his absence was as follows. He said, "You, my brothers, always leave me here alone in the camp. Yesterday several shepherds came, and forcibly carried me away. They kept me awake all night. They tied these shells round my neck and made me dance. They also made me drive cattle round and round. I had no rest all night. They also shewed me *hiras* and *manis*."

Lelha's brothers eagerly enquired, "Where did you see the *hiras* and *manis*? Come, show us the place at once." Lelha replied, "We must first buy food for the *hiras* and *manis*." So they went to the bazaar to buy food for the *hiras* and *manis*. Lelha first bought two goats, and his brothers abused him, and said, "Will *hiras* and *manis* eat these?" Some one of them said, "Slap him." Another said, "Do not slap him, they may perhaps eat them." Then he bought a pair of shoes, at which again they reviled him. Then he bought two ropes, when they again reviled him. Lastly he purchased two bundles of grass, and having provided these necessary articles, they went and hired a boat. The horses of the four brothers were dead, so they had to proceed on foot to where the boat lay.

After sailing for some time they reached an island, and landed. They quickly found the house of the *Indarpuri Kuri*. It was closed by a large stone lying over the entrance. Lelha ordered his brothers to remove it, but they were displeased and said, "How do you expect to find *hiras* and *manis* under this stone." Lelha said, "Truly, my brothers, they are under the stone." He pressed them to attempt the removal of the stone, so they, and others to the number of fifty tried their strength but the stone seemed immovable. Then Lelha said, "Stand by, and allow me to try." So putting to his hand, he easily removed it, and revealed the entrance to the mansion of the *Indarpuri Kuri*. His brothers were so astounded at the strength he displayed that they lost the power of speech.

Lelha then said to his brothers, "Take one of these ropes, and bind it round me, and lower me down, and when you feel me shaking the rope, then quickly pull me up. I go to find *hiras*." His brothers quickly bound the rope round his body, and he, taking the goats, the pair of shoes, and the bundles of grass, descended.

A short distance from where he reached the ground, he found a door, which was guarded by an elephant bound by the foot to a stake. To him he threw a bundle of grass and passed on. At the next door he found a tiger, likewise chained, and as he approached, it opened its jaws as if to devour him. To it, he gave a goat, and was allowed to pass. At the third door was a dog. He threw a shoe to it, and when the dog was engaged biting it, he passed through. Then he saw the *hira* sparkling upon the bosom of the sleeping *Indarpuri Kuri*.

Going near, he snatched it up, and fled. The dog, however, barred his exit but he threw the other shoe to it, and passed on. The tiger had devoured the goat he had given to it, and was now alert. To it he gave the other goat, and hurried on. The elephant then opposed him, but the remaining bundle of grass was sufficient to divert his attention, and he passed through the last door. Then violently shaking the rope his brothers speedily hauled him up.

Then they went to their boat, and rowed to another part of the island, where the Sinjo tree grew. They all climbed the tree, but Lelha plucked the five fruits on the branch to the South, while his brothers plucked a large number from the North side.

They then returned to their boat and rowed back to the place from which they had started. From there they went to the house of Lelha's bride. When she heard of their arrival she ordered refreshments to be prepared for them. Her servants also all came, and gave Lelha and his brothers oil, and sent them to bathe. On their return from bathing, their feet were washed by servants, and they were then taken into the house.

After they were seated Lelha's brothers began to whisper to each other, saying, "We do not know of what caste these people are, to whose house he has brought us to eat food. He will cause us to lose caste." Lelha heard what they were saying, and in explanation said, "Not so, brothers. This is my wife's house." They replied, "It is all right then." So they ate and drank heartily, and afterwards prepared to return home.

VI.

The journey was to be by boat. Lelha sent his brothers on ahead in one boat, and he and his wife followed in another. There was a distance of two or three kos between the boats.

Lelha's brothers as they sailed along came to a certain ghat at which a raja was bathing. He was raja of the country through which they were passing. He demanded from Lelha's brothers to know what they had in their boat. They replied, "We have *hiras* and *manis* with us." Then the raja said, "Shew them to me. You may be thieves." They replied, "No, they are inside these Sinjo fruits." The raja said, "Break one, I wish to see what they are like." So the brothers broke one, but nothing was found in it. Then the raja called his soldiers, and ordered them to bind the four brothers. So the soldiers seized and bound them, and carried them off to prison. Just then Lelha's boat arrived. He was in time to see his brothers pass within the prison doors. Having seen the four brothers in safe custody the raja returned to the bathing ghat, and seeing Lelha he demanded to know what he had in his boat. Lelha answered, "We have *hiras* and *manis* as our cargo." The raja then said, "Shew them to me, I would fain look upon them." Lelha said, "You wish to see *hiras* and *manis* without any trouble to yourself. If I show you them, what will you give me in return? There are *hiras* and *manis* in this Sinjo fruit." The raja replied, "Those who came before you deceived me. I have no doubt, but that you will do so also." Lelha said, "What will you give me? Make an offer, and I shall shew you them at once." The raja replied, "I have one daughter, her I will give to you, and along with her an estate, if there are *hiras* and *manis* in that Sinjo fruit, and if there are none in it, I will keep you prisoner all your lifetime." Lelha immediately broke one of the Sinjo fruits, and five *hiras* and *manis* rolled out. When the raja saw it he was confounded, but what could he do? According to his promise, he gave him his daughter and an estate.

The marriage ceremony being over, Lelha was invited to partake of the raja's hospitality, but he refused, saying, "If you set my brothers at liberty I shall eat, but not unless you do so." So the brothers were released, and taken to the bath. After they had bathed, their feet were washed, and they were led into the palace to the feast.

The brothers, after they were seated, began to whisper to each other, saying, "Whose house is this? Of what caste are the people? Does he wish to make us lose our caste?" But Lelha reassured them by saying, "Not so, my brothers. I have espoused the raja's daughter." Hearing this they were relieved, and all enjoyed the marriage feast.

VII.

Then they made preparations to continue their journey. Lelha again sent his four brothers first, and he followed with his two wives.

After a sail of a few hours they entered the territory of another raja, and came upon his bathing ghat. The raja was bathing there at the time, and the boat passing, he enquired what her cargo was. The brothers answered, "We have *hiras* and *manis* on board." The raja said, "I would see them." They replied, "They are in the boat following us." The raja was displeased with their answer, and ordered them to be seized as vagrants.

Lelha's boat came alongside the bathing ghat just as his four brothers were led off to prison, and the raja seeing it, asked Lelha what cargo he carried. Lelha replied, "Our cargo is *hiras* and *manis*." The raja begged Lelha to shew them to him, but he refused saying, "What will you give for a sight of them? Promise something, and you can see them." The raja said, "Of a truth, if you can shew me *hiras* and *manis* I will give you my daughter. I have one, a virgin, her I will give you, and I will also confer upon you an estate."

Then Lelha, seizing a Sinjo fruit, broke it, and out rolled five *hiras* and *manis*, which when the raja saw he marvelled greatly. He honourably fulfilled his engagement, and Lelha's marriage with his daughter was celebrated forthwith.

The wedding over Lelha was conducted to the bath, and afterwards invited to a banquet; but he declined saying, "So long as you detain my brothers in confinement, I cannot partake of your hospitality." So they were brought to the palace, and their feet bathed, and then ushered into the banqueting room. After they were seated they began to whisper to each other, "What caste do these people belong to, with whom he expects us to eat? Does he intend to make us break our caste?" Lelha hearing them, said, "Not so, my brothers. This is my father-in-law's house." Thus were their doubts removed, and they ate and drank with much pleasure.

VIII.

The journey homewards was resumed in the morning, the boats in the same order as previously.

Lelha's four brothers were envious of his good fortune, and on the way they talked about him, and decided that he must be put to death. They said, "How can we put him out of the way? If we do not make away with him, on our return home, he will be sure to secure the succession to our father's kingdom." Having come to this conclusion the next thing was, how could it be accomplished, for Lelha was far more powerful than they were. It was only by stratagem that they could hope to accomplish their purpose, so they said, "We will invite him to a feast and when he stands with a foot on either boat, before stepping into ours, we will push the boats apart and he will fall into the river and be drowned. We must get his wives to join in the plot, for without their aid we cannot carry it into execution." During the day they found means to communicate with Lelha's wives. They said to them, "We will make a feast on our boat. Make him come on board first, and when he has a foot on each boat you push yours back, and we will do the same to ours, and he will fall into the water, and be drowned. We are the sons of a raja, and our country is very large. We will take you with us and make you ranis." Lelha's wives pretended to agree to their proposal; but they afterwards told him all. They said, "Do as they wish, but you will not be drowned. We will remain faithful to you, and you will reach home before us."

So the four brothers prepared a sumptuous feast, and the boats were brought close to each other to enable Lelha and his wives to go on board. One of Lelha's wives tied a knot on his waist cloth, as a token that they would remain true to him. He then preceded them in going into the other boat, and just as he had a foot on each gunwale, the boats were pushed asunder, and Lelha fell into the water. Having thus got rid, as they thought, of Lelha, the brothers made all possible speed homewards.

IX.

At the bottom of the river a bell sprang into existence, and Lelha was found lying asleep in it. Then he awoke and sat up, and loosening the knot which his wife had tied on his waist cloth, said, "Oh! *Indarpuri Kuri*, give me at once food and drink, tobacco and fire," and on the instant his wants were supplied. So he ate and drank, and was refreshed. Then he prepared his pipe, and when he had lit it he said, "Oh! *Indarpuri Kuri*, give me a fully equipped horse that will carry me home before the tobacco in this pipe is consumed." The last word had scarcely escaped his lips when a horse stood beside him. It was a fierce animal, of a blue colour, and no fly could alight on its skin. It was fully equipped, and impatient to start. Lelha, still smoking his pipe, mounted, and his steed at one bound cleared the river, although it was seven or eight kos broad, and flying like the wind, landed him at home before the tobacco in his pipe was consumed.

The *hiras* and *manis* were in the possession of Lelha's wives. His brothers wheedled them into giving them up, saying they will be safer with us.

Lelha went to his mother's house and said to her, "Tell no one of my being here." He had alighted from his horse on the outskirts of the city, and returned it to the *Indarpuri Kuri*.

A period of ten days elapsed before Lelha's brothers and his wives arrived. The latter declined to accompany the former at once to the raja's palace. They said, "Let your mothers come, and conduct us, as is usual when a bride enters her husband's house." The two elder ranis then came, and the four sons went to the raja's flower garden and hung the *hiras* and *manis* on the branches of the trees, and the whole countryside was instantly lighted up by the sheen of the precious stones. The saying of the Koema *Jugi* was fulfilled to the letter.

Lelha also sent his mother to welcome his wives, but when the elder ranis saw her coming, they reviled her and drove her away. They would not permit her to come near. She returned home weeping. "You told me," she said, "to go and welcome your wives, and I have been abused. When will you learn wisdom?" Lelha ran into the house, and brought a ring, and giving it to his mother, said, "Take this ring, and place it in the lap of one of them." She took the ring, and gave it to one of Lelha's wives, and immediately they all rose, and followed her laughing, to their new home.

The elder ranis went and informed their sons of what had happened, but they said, "They are Lelha's wives. What can we do?"

X.

The *Indarpuri Kuri* whom Lelha had robbed of her *hira* now awoke, and at once missed her precious jewel. She knew that Lelha had stolen it from her, and summoning her army to her standard marched upon Lelha's father's capital, to which she laid siege, and before many hours had elapsed, the raja was a prisoner in her hands.

This *Indarpuri Kuri* said to him, "Will you give up the *hiras* and *manis*, or will you fight?" The raja sent the following message to his four sons, "Will you fight to retain possession of the *hiras* and *manis*, or will you deliver them up?" They were afraid, so they gave answer, "We will not. Lelha knows all about the *hiras* and *manis*. We do not."

The raja then sent and called Lelha, and enquired, "Will you shew fight, Lelha, or will you give up the *hiras* and *manis*?" Lelha replied, "I will fight. I will not part with the *hiras* and *manis*. I obtained them only after much painful toil, so I cannot deliver them up. Ask them to agree to delay hostilities for a short time, but inform them that Lelha will fight."

Lelha hurried to the further end of the garden, and taking the hair of the first *Indarpuri Kuri* in his hand said, "Oh! *Indarpuri Kuri*. Give me an army four times stronger than the one brought against me, so that I may make short work of my enemies." Immediately an army of 44,000 men stood in military array, awaiting his orders. The two armies joined battle, and Lelha discomfited the host of the *Indarpuri Kuri*, and she herself became his prize. She became his wife, and returned no more to her cavernous home in the solitary island. Lelha thus became the husband of four wives.

Then the raja called his five sons together and said, "In my estimation Lelha is the one best qualified to became raja of this kingdom. I therefore resign all power and authority into his hands." Lelha replied, "Yes, father, you have judged righteously. My brothers have caused me much distress. First, they pushed off the raised platform in your flower garden, but of that I did not inform you. Then they caused me, who was the finder of the *hiras* and *manis*, to fall into the river. You saw how they refused to fight, and threw all the responsibility upon me. They have used me spitefully. They have tried to make a cat's paw of me."

So Lelha was raja of all the country, and his brothers were his servants. One was in charge of Lelha's pipe and tobacco, another ploughed his fields, and the other two had like menial offices assigned to them.

1 Lelha in Santali means foolish.

2 Diamonds.

3 A mythical gem, said to be found in the heads of certain snakes.

4 Celestial horses.

5 Celestial Maiden.

6 Ægle Marmelos, Correa.

The Story of Sindura Gand Garur.

In a certain village there lived a mother and her son. The boy tended goats in the forest. One day he found a spot of ground, where he thought rice would grow well. So he went home, and asked his mother to give him some seed to sow there. She said, "If you sow rice there it will all be destroyed. The elephants, or the wild jungle cattle, will eat it." But he begged so hard that at length she gave him some seed rice, which he sowed on the small plot of ground in the jungle. It sprang up and grew luxuriantly. Every day he drove his goats there, and spent the long hours in driving the birds and insects away from his little farm.

When the rice had grown to a good height the raja's son with his companion came and set up a mark near by at which they shot with their bows and arrows. The orphan boy was asked to join them, which he did, and so accurate was his aim, that he hit the mark every time he shot. The raja's son and his companion were astonished to see such good shooting, and they said, "The fatherless boy hits the mark every time."

The boy ran home to his mother weeping, and said, "Oh! mother, where is my father?" To keep him from grieving, she told a lie. "Your father," she said, "has gone on a visit to his relations."

The next day after he had again shown great skill with the bow and arrow the raja's son and his companion said, "The fatherless boy hits the mark every time." Hearing this he again went home weeping, and said to his mother, "Oh! mother, where is my father?" She replied, "He has gone to visit his friends." Every day the boy came crying to his mother asking where his father was, so at last she told him. She said, "Your father, child, was carried away on the horns of a *Gand Garur* 1."

The boy then said to his mother, "Prepare me some flour. I will go in search of him." His mother tried to dissuade him, saying, "Where can you go in such a jungle as this?" He, however, insisted, and she prepared flour for him, and he set out.

After travelling many hours he entered the primeval forest, and presently darkness came upon him. After a short time he came to the dwelling of *Huti2 Budhi,* and requested permission to pass the night there. This was accorded to him, and he lay down and fell asleep. During the night he was awakened by the *Huti Budhi* eating his bow and arrows. He called out to her "Oh! old woman, What have you been nibbling at since evening?" The *Huti Budhi* replied, "It is only some roasted grain, which I brought a while ago from the house of the Chief."

In a short time the nibbling sound was again heard, and he again enquired what she was eating. She returned the same answer as before. "Oh! my son, it is only roasted grain which the chief's people gave me." He did not know that all the time she was eating his bow and arrows.

When morning dawned he requested her to give him his weapons, and on his attempting to string the bow it broke in his hands. The *Huti Budhi* had eaten the heart out of the wood, and had left only the outer shell. He left her house planning revenge.

During the day he had an iron bow and iron arrows made. All was iron like the arrow heads. In the evening he returned to sleep at the *Huti Budhi's* house.

During the night he heard the *Huti Budhi* trying to nibble his bow and arrows. So he enquired what she was doing. The answer she gave was, "Do you think the *Huti Budhi* can eat iron."

When morning dawned he demanded his bow and arrows, and received them uninjured, but the lower part of the *Huti Budhi's* face was all swollen. She had been trying to eat the iron bow and arrows. Her lodger strung his bow, and having saluted her, went his way.

As he journeyed he entered another unexplored forest in the midst of which he discovered a lake, to which all the birds and beasts resorted to quench their thirst. He obtained this information by an examination of its banks, on which he saw the footprints of the various beasts and birds. He now took some flour from his bag, and having moistened it with water made a hearty meal, and then sat down to wait for evening.

As the sun went down the denizens of the forest began to come to the lake to drink. They came in quick succession, and as each made its appearance, he sang assurance to it, that he harboured no evil design against it.

The quail led the way, and to it he sang,

> "Oh! quail, you need not fear to drink,
> I'll not harm you, I you assure;
> But I will slay on this lake's brink,
> Cruel Sindura Gand Garur.

He sang in a similar strain to each bird as it came, naming it by its name.

At length the *Gand Garur* alighted on the edge of the lake to drink, and he at once drew his bow, and sent an arrow to its heart, for he had seen the dried and shrivelled corpse of his father still adhering to its horns. The *Gand Garur* being dead, he detached what remained of his parent's body from its horns, and taking it in his arms pressed it to his bosom and wept bitterly.

As he wept, *Bidi* and *Bidhati* descended from the sky and asked him the reason of his sorrow. So he told them all. They spoke words of comfort to him, and said, "Dip your gamcha cloth in the lake, and cover the corpse with it. And don't you cry, rather bathe and cook some food. And do not cook for one only, but prepare portions for two. And when the food is ready, you partake of one portion, and set the other aside. Then tap your father on the back and say, 'Rise father, here is your food.'" He did as his kind friends bade him, and the dead came to life again. The father sat up and said, "Oh! my son, what a lengthened sleep I have had." The son replied, "A sleep? you must be demented, you were pierced through by the horns of the *Gand Garur*, and your dried carcase was adhering to them. See I have killed it. It is lying here. *Bidi* and *Bidhati* instructed me how to proceed, and I have brought you to life again.

So they returned joyfully home singing the praises of *Bidi* and *Bidhati*.

1 A mythical bird which figures largely in Indian folk lore.

2 Huti is the name given by Santals to a certain timber boring insect. Budhi is an old woman.

The Tiger and Ulta's Mother.

A tiger cub was in the habit of playing under the shade of a certain tree, in which was a crane's nest with a young one in it. The parent cranes brought frogs and lizards to their young one, and what it could not eat it used to throw down to the young tiger, and in this way the two became greatly attached to each other. After a time the tigress died, and left the cub alone in the world. The young crane felt much pity for its afflicted friend, and could not bear the thought of itself being in a better position. So one day it said to the tiger, "Let us kill my mother." The tiger replied, "Just as you please. I cannot say do it, nor can I say do not do it." When the mother crane came to give its young one food, the latter set upon her and killed her. The friendship between the two increased so that they could not be separated from each other. Day and night they spent in each other's society.

After a time the two said, "Come let us make a garden, and plant in it turmeric." So they prepared a piece of ground, and the crane brought roots of turmeric from a distance. They then discussed the matter as to which part of the crop each would take. The crane said to the tiger, "You, my brother, choose first." The tiger said, "If I must speak first, I will take the leaves." Then, said the crane, "I will take the roots." Having settled this point to their satisfaction, they began to plant. The tiger dug holes, and the crane put in the roots, and covered them over with earth.

A year passed, and they again said to each other, "Which of us will take the roots, and which the leaves?" The tiger said, "I will take the leaves." The crane replied, "I will take the roots." So they began to dig up the plants, and cutting the leaves from the roots, placed each by themselves. The tiger collected an immense bulk of leaves, and the crane a large heap of roots. This done each surveyed the other's portion. That of the crane was of a beautiful, reddish tinge, and excited the envy of the tiger, who said to the crane, "Give me half of yours, and I will give you half of mine." The crane refused, saying, "I will not share with you. Why did you at first chose the leaves? I gave you your choice." The tiger insisted, but the crane was obdurate, and before long they were quarrelling as if they had been lifelong enemies. The crane seeing it was being worsted in the wrangle, flew in the face of the tiger, and pecked its eyes, so that it became blind. It then flew away, and left the tiger lamenting its sad fate. Having lost its sight it could not find its way about, so remained there weeping.

One day, hearing the voice of a man near by, the tiger called out, "Oh! man, are you a doctor?" The man stupefied with fear stared at the tiger, and gave no reply. The tiger again said, "Oh! man, why do you not reply to my question? Although you are a human being, have you no pity?" The man then said, "Oh! renowned hero, what did you ask me? I am terror stricken, so did not reply. You may devour me." The tiger replied, "If I had wished to kill you, I could have done so, but I mean you no harm." The tiger again asked the man if he possessed a knowledge of medicine, but he replied, "I do not." The tiger then asked, "Is there one amongst you who does know?" The man replied, "Yes." The tiger enquired, "Who is he?" The man said, "There is a certain widow with two sons, the name of one of whom is Ulta, who possesses a knowledge of medicine, she will be able to cure you." Having given the tiger this information the man went away.

The tiger went to the house of Ulta's mother, and hid himself behind a hedge. He said within himself, "When I hear any one call Ulta then I will go forward." Shortly after the tiger arrived Ulta's mother called Ulta, "Ulta, come to your supper." Then the tiger ran hastily forward, and cried, "Oh! Ulta's mother, Oh! Ulta's mother." But she was afraid, and exclaimed, "This tiger has done for us to-day." The tiger said to the woman, "Do you know medicine?" She replied, "Yes, Wait till I bring it." So hastily running out she said to her neighbours, "A tiger has come to my house. He is blind, and wishes me to cure his blindness." The neighbours said to her, "Give him some of the juice of the Akauna1 tree. It will increase his blindness." So she quickly brought Akauna juice, and giving it to the tiger, said, "Go to some dense jungle and apply it to your eyes. Do not apply it here, or it will have no effect. Take it away. We are about to sit down to supper, and then my children will go to sleep. The medicine will cause you pain at first, but it will effect a complete cure."

The tiger hurried away to the jungle, and poured the akauna juice into his eyes. The pain it caused was as if his eyeballs were being torn out. He tossed himself about in agony, and at last struck his head against a tree. In a short time, his blindness was gone. He could see everything plainly, and was delighted beyond expression.

One day several traders were passing along a pathway through the jungle in which the tiger hunted. He was lying concealed watching for prey, and when the traders were passing he jumped out upon them. Seeing the tiger they fled, and left behind them their silver, and gold, and brass vessels. The tiger collected all and carried them to Ulta's mother's house, and presenting them to her said, "All this I give to you, for through you I have again seen the earth. Had it not been for you, who knows whether I should ever have been cured or not." Ulta's mother was delighted with the generosity of the tiger. He had made her rich at once. But she was anxious to get rid of him, and said "Go away. May you always find a living somewhere." So the tiger returned to the jungle again.

Sometime afterwards the tiger was minded to take a wife, and sought his old friend Ulta's mother. On arriving at her house he called out, "Oh! Ulta's mother, where are you? Are you in your house?" She replied, "Who are you?" The tiger answered, "It is I, the forest hero. You cured my blindness." So Ulta's mother came out of her house, and said, "Wherefore, Sir, have you come here?" "I wish you," replied the tiger, "to find a bride for me." Ulta's mother said, "Come to-morrow and I will tell you. Do not stay to-day." So the tiger left.

Ulta's mother then went to her neighbours and said, "The tiger has put me in a great difficulty. He wishes me to find a bride for him." They said to her, "Is he not blind?" She replied, "No. He sees now, and it is that, which distresses me. What can I do?" They said, "Get a bag, and order him to go into it, and then tie up the mouth tightly, and tell him to remain still. Say to him, If you move, or make a noise, I will not seek a bride for you. And when you have him tied securely in the bag, call us." The next day the tiger appeared, and Ulta's mother told him to get into the bag, and allow her to tie it. So he went in, and she tied the bag's mouth, and said, "You must not move, lie still, or I shall not be your go-between." Having secured him, Ulta's mother called her neighbours, who came armed with clubs, and began to beat the helpless animal. He called out, "Oh! Ulta's mother, what are you doing?" She said, "Keep quiet. They are beating the marriage drums. Lie still a little longer." The tiger remained motionless, while they continued to beat him. At length they said, "He must be dead now, let us throw him out." So they carried him to a river, and having thrown him in, returned home.

The current bore the tiger far down the river, but at length he stranded in a cove. A short time afterwards a tigress came down to the river to drink and seeing the bag, and thinking it might contain something edible she seized it and dragged it up on to the bank. The tigress then cut the bag open with her teeth, and the tiger sprang out, exclaiming, "Of a truth she has given me a bride. Ulta's mother has done me a good turn, and I shall remember her as long as I live." The tiger and the tigress being of one mind on the subject agreed never to separate.

One day the two tigers said "Come let us go and pay a visit to Ulta's mother, who has proved so helpful to us. As we cannot go empty handed, let us rob some one to get money to take with us." So they went and lay in wait near a path which passed through the forest in which they lived. Presently a party of merchants came up, and the tigers with a loud roar sprang from their ambush on to the road. The merchants seeing them, fled, and left behind them all their property in money and cloth. Those they carried to Ulta's mother. When she saw the tigers approaching her throat became dry through terror.

Before entering the court-yard they called out to Ulta's mother announcing their approach. Ulta's mother addressed the tiger thus, "Why do you come here frightening one in this way?" The tiger replied, "There is no fear. It is I who am afraid of you. Why should you dread my coming? It was you who found this partner for me. Do you not yet know me?" Ulta's mother replied, "What can you do Sir? Do you not remember that we give and receive gifts on the Karam festival day? On the days for giving and receiving, we give and receive. Now, that you are happily wedded, may you live in peace and comfort; but do not come here again."

The tiger then gave Ulta's mother a large amount of money and much cloth, after which the two tigers took their leave, and Ulta's mother entered her house loaded with rupees and clothing.

1 Calotropis gigantea, R. Br.

The Greatest Cheat of Seven.

A great cheat married the cheating sister of seven cheats. One day his father-in-law and seven brothers-in-law came on a visit to his house. After conversing with them for a little, he invited them to accompany him to the river to bathe. He carried a fishing rod with him, and on arriving at the river cast his line into a pool, saying, "Now, fish, if you do not instantly repair to my house, I shall not be able to speak well of you." This he said to deceive the others, as before leaving home he had given a fish to his wife telling her to prepare it for dinner. When seated at table he said to his guests, "the fish we are now eating is the one I, in your presence, ordered to proceed from the river to my house this forenoon." They were greatly astonished at the wonderful properties possessed by the fishing rod, and expressed a desire to purchase it, and offered to pay five rupees for it. He accepted their offer, and they carried the wonderful fishing rod home with them.

Next day they arranged to go a-fishing. They cast the line into a pool as they had seen the cheat do, and said, "Now fish, if you do not repair at once to our home we shall not be able to speak well of you." Having bathed they returned home, and asked to see the fish. Their wives said, "What fish? You gave us no fish. We have seen no fish. Where did you throw it down?" They now knew that their sister's husband was a cheat, so they decided to go and charge him with having deceived them.

The cheat had notice of their coming, and quickly taking his dog with him went to hunt. He caught a hare and bringing it home gave it to his wife, and said, "When we reach the end of the street on our way home from hunting, you make the dog stand near the house with the dead hare in his mouth."

He invited his visitors to accompany him for an hour's hunting, saying, "Come, let us go and kill a hare for dinner." So they went to the jungle, and presently started a hare. The cheat threw a stone at his dog, and frightened it so that it ran home. He called after it, "If you do not catch and take that hare home, it will not be well for you." He then said to his friends, "Come, let us return, we will find the dog there with the hare before us." They replied, "We doubt it much." "There is no mistake about it," he said, "We are certain to find both dog and hare." On reaching home they found the dog standing waiting for them with a hare in his mouth.

His brothers-in-law were astonished beyond measure at the sagacity of the dog, and they said, "Sell this dog to us, we will pay a good price for it." He demanded ten rupees, which they gladly paid. So they returned home, and said nothing to him about his having cheated them in the matter of the fishing rod.

One day, taking the dog with them, they went to hunt. It caught five hares, and its masters were greatly delighted with its performance.

After this the cheat's house was accidentally burnt, and he gathering the ashes together, set out for the bazaar, there to sell them. On the way he fell in with a party of merchants who had a large bag full of silver with them. They enquired what his bag contained, to which he replied, "Gold." They agreed to pass the night in the same encampment, so having partaken of their evening meal, they lay down to sleep. At midnight the merchants rose, and exchanged the bags, and then lay down again. The cheat saw them, and chuckled within himself. In the morning the merchants made haste to leave, as they feared the cheat might find out the theft of his bag. The cheat asked them before they left to help him to lift his bag on to his bullock's back, saying, "It was to receive assistance from you that I encamped here last night." So having helped him to load his bullock they hurried away lest they should be caught. The cheat carried his treasure home, but being unable to count so much money borrowed a measure from his father-in-law, and found he had four maunds of silver.

On returning the measure he sent along with it five seers of silver, saying, "For the ashes of my house I received four maunds of silver, if you reduce your houses to ashes and sell them, you will obtain very much more." So they foolishly burnt their houses, and collecting the ashes went to the bazaar to dispose of them. The merchants to whom they offered them directed them to go to the washermen, saying, "They will possibly buy." But they also refused, and they were compelled to return home without having effected a sale. They vowed vengeance on the cheat, and set out to find him.

When they reached his house the cheat was on the point of starting on a journey. After mutual salutations he said, "I have just killed my second wife. I go to receive eight maunds of silver for her corpse. Dead bodies bring high prices." They said to him, "How about the ashes? We could not sell them." He replied, "You did not go far enough from home. Had you gone to a distance you would have made a good bargain."

The cheat's youngest wife having died he washed the body, and anointed it with oil. He then put it in a large bag, and loaded it on the back of a bullock, and set out. On the way he came to a field of wheat, into which he drove the animal, and then hid himself near by. The owner of the field finding the bullock eating his wheat, beat it unmercifully with a cudgel. The cheat then came from his hiding place, and said, "Have you not done wrong in beating my bullock? If you have killed my wife, where will you flee to? I fell behind, and for that reason my ox got into your field. My wife, whom I have newly married, is weak and unable to go on foot, so I put her into a bag to carry her home on my bullock."

Having opened the bag the wife was found dead, and her assailant stood self convicted of her murder. He gave her husband six maunds of rupees as hush money, so the cheat burnt the corpse and returned home laden with spoil.

The cheat next sent for his brothers-in-law, and shewing them the money, said, "I killed my second wife, and got all this money by selling the corpse." They enquired, "Who are the people who buy dead bodies?" He replied, "They reside in the Rakas country."

Then the seven brothers killed each his youngest wife, and carried the bodies to a distant country to dispose of them. When the people of that country knew the object for which they had come they said to them, "What sort of men are you hawking corpses about the towns and villages? You must be the worst, or else most stupid of men." Hearing this the brothers were dismayed, and began to take in the situation. They perceived that the cheat had again deceived them, and they retraced their steps homewards bitterly lamenting their folly. On reaching their village they cremated the remains of their wives, and from that day had no more dealings with the cheat.

The Story of Two Princesses.

A certain raja had two daughters, who were in the habit of amusing themselves out side of the palace walls. One day they saw a crow flying towards them with a ripe Terel1 fruit in his beak. They then said to each other, "What fruit is it? It looks nice and sweet." The crow let the fruit fall in front of them. They ran and picked it up, and ate it. It tasted deliciously sweet. Then they said, "From whence did the crow bring such a good fruit?" Then they remembered the direction from which they had seen it coming, and said, "If we go this way we shall find it." So they went, but it was only after they had travelled a great distance from home that they found the Terel tree with the ripe luscious fruit.

The elder of the two girls climbed up into the tree, and shook down a large quantity of the fruit. They then feasted to their heart's content. Presently they began to feel thirsty, and the elder said to the younger, "You remain here while I go to drink, and I will also bring you water in a leaf cup." Having said this she went away to the tank, and her sister remained under the Terel tree. The day was extremely hot, and they were very thirsty.

The elder having quenched her thirst was returning carrying water for her sister in a cup made of the leaves of a Terel tree, when a bhut came flying along, and fell into the cup of water. Presently she became aware that there was a hole in the bottom of her cup through which all the water had run out. What could she do now? There was no help for it but to return to the tank, make another leaf cup, and filling it with water return to her sister. As she was returning with the cup full of water the bhut again came flying up, and entering the water passed through the leaf, making a hole by which all the water escaped.

Again she made a leaf cup, and having filled it with water was returning when the bhut again came, and destroyed her cup, and caused her to lose the water. In this way she was detained till very late.

A raja who happened to be in the vicinity saw a beautiful girl carrying water in a leaf cup, and a bhut come and make a hole in the cup, so that it soon became empty. Having seen this several times repeated, he drew near, and feasted his eyes on her beauty. Then he carried her away to his palace, where they were joined in wedlock, and the princess, now the rani, cooked the food for herself and her husband.

The younger princess remained near the Terel tree, and although she had given up hope of again meeting her sister, still she continued to wait. At length a herd of Hanuman monkeys came to feed upon the Terel fruit. When the girl saw them coming she was terrified and crept into the hollow of the tree. The monkeys with the exception of an old frail one, climbed into the tree and began to eat the fruit. The old monkey remained below and picked up the fruit shells which the others threw down.

The old monkey having noticed the girl hiding in the hollow of the tree called to the others, "Throw me down some. If you do not I shall not share the *Setke chopot* I have found." The monkeys in the tree said, "Do not give him any. He is deceiving us. When his hunger is satisfied he will run and leave us." So no fruit was thrown down to him, and he was forced to be content with the shells. The monkeys in the tree having fared sumptuously, left. The old monkey waited till they were out of sight, and then entered the hollow of the tree, where the girl was, and ate her up. He then went to the tank to drink, and afterwards went in the direction of the raja's garden, on reaching which he lay down and died. One of the gardeners finding him dead threw him on the dunghill.

From the place where the monkey decayed a gourd sprang, and grew, and bore a fruit which ripened. One day a jugi, when on his rounds begging, saw this fruit and plucking it took it away with him. Out of the shell he made a banjo, which when played upon emitted wonderful music. The words which seemed to proceed from the banjo were as follows:

Ripe terels, ripe terels, Oh! Sister mine.

Went in search of water, Oh! Sister mine.

Raja and Rani they became.

Seven hundred monkeys old,

Ate me up, ate me up. Oh! Sister mine.

The jugi was greatly pleased with the music of his new banjo, and determined to take it with him when he went a begging. So one day he set out with his banjo the music of which so pleased the people that they gave him large gifts of money and clothes. In course of time he arrived at the palace where the elder sister was now rani, and, being admitted, began to play on his banjo. The instrument again produced most wonderful music. It seemed to wail as follows:

Ripe terels, ripe terels, Oh! Sister mine.

Went in search of water, Oh! Sister mine.

Raja and Rani they became.

Seven hundred monkeys old,

Ate me up, ate me up. Oh! Sister mine.

Having listened to the music the rani said, "It is wonderfully sweet," and she fancied she heard her sister's voice in every note. She thought it possible that it was she who sang in the banjo, and she desired to obtain possession of it. So she invited the jugi to pass the night in the palace, saying, I would hear more of this entrancing music." The jugi listened to the words of the rani and agreed to remain till morning. So the rani made much of him with the intention of at length obtaining possession of his banjo. She caused a goat to be killed, and she cooked a splendid supper for the jugi, who finding the food so toothsome ate heartily. Wine was not withheld, and the jugi being in a festive frame of mind drank deeply, so that he soon lay as one dead. The rani took the banjo, and placed another in its stead. She then threw filth over the unconscious jugi and retired to her own apartment.

The jugi on awaking before sunrise found himself in a pitiable plight. He felt so thoroughly disgusted with himself that, hastily picking up his staff, cloth, and banjo, he fled with the utmost possible speed from the palace. When dawn broke he saw that the banjo he had was not his own, and although he felt keenly its loss he was too much ashamed of the condition he had been in to go back to seek it.

The rani hid the jugi's banjo in her own room, because she knew her sister to be in it. Whenever the raja and rani went out to walk the girl left the banjo and having bathed and dressed her hair, cooked the family meal, and then returned to the banjo. This happened so often that at last, it came to the knowledge of the raja that a fairy lived in the banjo, and when the way was clear used to come out and prepare food for the rani and himself. So he determined to lie in wait for the fairy cook. He then sent the rani somewhere on an errand, and hid himself in a corner of the room from whence he could see the banjo. In a short time the princess emerged from the banjo, and began to dress her hair, and anoint herself with oil, after which she cooked rice. She divided the food into three portions, one of which she ate. As she was about to re-enter the banjo the raja sprang out and caught hold of her. She exclaimed, "Chi! Chi! you may be a Hadi, or you may be a Dom." The raja replied, "Chi! Chi! whether I be a Dom, or a Hadi, from to-day you and I are one."

1 Diospyros tomentosa.

Seven Brothers and their Sister.

In a certain village there lived seven brothers and a sister. Their family was wealthy. Their father was dead. The brothers agreed to dig a tank so that whatever happened their name would continue. So they began the work, but although they dug deep they found no water. Then they said to each other, "Why is there no water?" While they were speaking thus among themselves a jugi gosae on his rounds, came to the tank in the hope of finding water, but he was disappointed. The seven brothers on seeing the jugi gosae went and sat down near him, and said, "We have been working for many days, and have dug so deep, still we have not reached water. You, who are a jugi gosae, tell us why water does not come." He replied, "Unless you give a gift you will never get water." They enquired, "What should we give." The jugi gosae replied, "Not gold, or silver, or an elephant, or a horse, but you have a sister?" They said, "Yes, we have one sister." He replied, "Then make a gift of her to the spirit of the tank." The girl was betrothed, and her family had received the amount that had been fixed as her price. The brothers argued thus, "We have laboured so long to make a name for ourselves, but have not found water, so where is our name? If we do not sacrifice our sister we shall never obtain the fulfilment of our wishes, let us all agree to it." So they all said, "Agreed," but the youngest did not fully approve of their design.

In the evening they said to their mother, "Let our sister wash her clothes, dress her hair, and put on all her ornaments to-morrow when she brings us our breakfast to the tank." They did not, however, enlighten their mother as to why they desired their sister to be so careful with her toilet.

The following day the mother addressed her daughter as follows, "Oh! my daughter, your brothers yesterday said to me, let the daughter, when she brings us our breakfast come with clean clothes, her hair dressed and all her ornaments on. So as it is nearly time, go and dress, and put on all your ornaments, and take your brothers' breakfast to where they are working." She complied with her mother's order, and set out for the tank, dressed in her best with all her ornaments on, carrying boiled rice in a new basket.

When she arrived at the tank her brothers said to her, "Oh! daughter, set down the basket under yonder tree." She did so, and the brothers came to where she was. They then said to her, "Go bring us water from the tank to drink." She took her water-pot under her arm, and went into the tank, but did not at once find water. Presently, however, she saw the sheen of water in the centre, and went to fill her pitcher, but she could not do so, as the water rose so rapidly. The tank was soon full to the brim, and the girl was drowned.

The brothers having seen their sister perish, went home. Their mother enquired, "Oh! my sons, where is the daughter?" They replied, "We have given her to the tank. A certain jugi gosae said to us, 'Unless you offer up your sister you will never get water'." On hearing this she loudly wailed the loss of her daughter. Her sons strove to mitigate her grief by saying, "Look mother, we undertook the excavation of the tank to perpetuate our name, and to gain the fruit of a meritorious work. And unless there be water in the tank for men and cattle to drink, where is the perpetuation of our name? By our offering up the daughter the tank is full to overflowing. So the cattle can now quench their thirst, and travellers, when they encamp near by and drink the water, will say, 'The excavators of this tank deserve the thanks of all. We, and others who pass by are recipients of their bounty. Their merit is indeed great'." In this way with many such like arguments they sought to allay their mother's grief.

Right in the centre of the tank, where the girl was drowned, there sprang up an Upel flower the purple, sheen of which filled the beholder with delight.

It has already been stated that the girl had been betrothed, and that her family had received the money for her. The day appointed for the marriage arrived, and the bridegroom's party with drums, elephants and horses, set out for the bride's house. On arrival they were informed that she had left her home, and that all efforts to trace her had proved fruitless. So they returned home greatly disappointed. It so happened that their way lay past the tank in which the girl had been sacrificed, and the bridegroom, from his palki, saw the Upel flower in the centre. As he wished to possess himself of it, he ordered his bearers to set down the palki, and stepping out prepared to swim out to pluck the flower. His companions tried to dissuade him, but as he insisted he was permitted to enter the water. He swam to within a short distance of the flower, but as he stretched out his hand to pluck it, the Upel flower, moving away, said, "Chi! Chi! Chi! Chi! You may be either a Dom or a Hadi, do not touch me." The bridegroom replied, "Not so. Are not we two one?" He made another effort to seize the flower, but it again moved away, saying, "Chi! Chi! Chi! Chi! you may be a Dom or a Hadi, so do not touch me." To which he replied, "Not so. You and I are one." He swam after it again, but the flower eluded his grasp, and said, "Chi! Chi! Chi! Chi! You may be a Dom, or you may be a Hadi, so do not touch me." He said, "Not so. You and I are bride and bridegroom for ever." Then the Upel flower allowed itself to be plucked, and the bridegroom returned to his company bearing it with him.

He entered his palki and the cortege started. They had not proceeded far before the bearers were convinced that the palki was increasing in weight. They said, "How is it that it is now so heavy? A short time ago it was light." So they pushed aside the panel, and beheld the bride and bridegroom sitting side by side. The marriage party on hearing the glad news rejoiced exceedingly. They beat drums, shouted, danced, and fired off guns. Thus they proceeded on their homeward way.

When the bridegroom's family heard the noise, they said, one to the other "Sister, they have arrived." Then they went forth to meet the bridegroom, and brought them in with great rejoicing. The bride was she who had been the Upel flower, and was exceedingly beautiful. In form she was both human and divine. The village people, as well as the marriage guests, when they saw her, exclaimed, "What a beautiful bride! She is the fairest bride that we have seen. She has no peer." Thus they all praised her beauty.

It so happened that in the meantime the mother and brothers of the girl had become poor. They were reduced to such straits as to be compelled to sell firewood for a living. So one day the brothers went to the bridegroom's village with firewood for sale. They offered it to one and another, but no one would buy. At last some one said, "Take it to the house in which the marriage party is assembled. They may require it." So the brothers went there, and asked, "Will you buy firewood?" They replied, "Yes. We will take it." Some one informed the bride, that some men from somewhere had brought firewood for sale. So she went out, and at once recognised her brothers, and said to them, "Put down your loads," and when they had done so she placed beds for them to sit on, and brought them water; but they did not know that she was their sister, as she was so greatly changed. Then she gave them vessels of oil, and said, "Go bathe, for you will dine here to-day." So they took the oil, and went to bathe, but they were so hungry that they drank the oil on the way. So they bathed, and returned to the house. She then brought them water to wash their hands, and they sat down in a row to eat. The bride gave her youngest brother food on a brass plate, because he had not approved of what had been done to her, but to the others she gave it on leaf plates.

They had only eaten one handful of rice when the girl placed herself in front of them, and putting a hand upon her head, began to weep bitterly. She exclaimed, "Oh! my brothers, you had no pity upon me. You threw me away as an offering to the tank. You saw me lost, and then went home." When the brothers heard this they felt as if their breasts were torn open. If they looked up to heaven, heaven was high. Then they saw an axe which they seized, and with it they struck the ground with all their might. It opened like the mouth of a large tiger, and the brothers plunged in. The girl caught the youngest brother by the hair to pull him up, but it came away in her hand, and they all disappeared into the bowels of the earth, which closed over them.

The girl held the hair in her hand and wept over it. She then planted it, and from it sprang the hair like Bachkom1 grass, and from that time Bachkom grass grows in the jungles.

The sister had pity on her youngest brother because he did not join heartily with the others in causing her death. So she tried to rescue him from the fate which was about to overtake him, but in this she failed, and he suffered for the sins of his brothers.

1 Ischœmum agustifolium, Hack.

The Story of Jhore.

There was a lad named Jhore, who herded goats, and every day while with his flock he saw a tiger and a lizard fight. The lizard always vanquished the tiger, and the latter after each encounter came to Jhore and said, "Which of us won?" Jhore through fear every time replied, "You won," and the tiger went away pleased.

One day Jhore said to his mother, give me some roasted matkom in a leaf, and put me into a bag and I will tell you something. So she wrapped up some matkom in a leaf, and Jhore crept into the bag and she tied its mouth. Then she said, "What is it, my son, which you wish to tell me?" Jhore replied, "Every day when I am tending my goats I see a tiger and a lizard fight, and the tiger is vanquished by the lizard. The tiger then comes to me and asks, 'which of us won?' Through fear I say, you won, then the tiger goes away satisfied."

While Jhore was relating the foregoing to his mother the tiger was listening at the door, and as he finished his story it rushed in, and seizing the bag carried it off to a dense unexplored forest, on a hill in the middle of which he placed it. Jhore was very uncomfortable, and was considering how he could best free himself from the bag. As he was hungry he was reminded of the matkom he had with him wrapped in a leaf, so he began to open it, and the dried leaf crackled. The tiger hearing the noise, asked what produced it. Jhore replied, "It is yesterday's lizard." The tidings of the presence of his mortal enemy so terrified the tiger that he exclaimed, "Stop, stop, Jhore. Do not release him. Let me first escape." After the tiger left Jhore rolled down the hill side, and away into a still denser forest, in an open spot of which he came to a stop. The fastening of the bag was loosed by this time, and Jhore crawled out. All round this open glade in which our hero found himself was dense forest never trodden by the foot of man, and tenanted by a herd of wild buffaloes. Jhore took up his residence there, and subsisted on the roasted matkom as long as it lasted.

Jhore in his explorations found a number of buffaloe calves left behind by their mothers who had gone to graze. He tended these daily, cleaning the place where they lived, and taking them to the water, where he washed them.

In this way a bond of friendship was established between him and the wild buffaloe calves.

Before the buffaloe cows left for their grazing grounds in the mornings the calves said, "You stay away till so late at night that, we are almost famished before you return. Leave some milk with us, so that when hungry we may drink it." So they left a supply of milk with them, which they gave to Jhore. He took such care of his charges that he soon became a great favourite with them.

Matters went on thus for many days till at last the buffaloe cows said among themselves, "We must watch for, and catch whoever it is who keeps our calves so clean." So a very powerful wild buffaloe was appointed to lie in wait, but he missed seeing Jhore when he led the calves to the water and bathed them, and cleaned and swept out their stall. The next day another took his place, but he succeeded no better. The calves were taken to the water, bathed, brought back, and their stall cleaned and swept as usual without his seeing who did it. When the others returned in the evening he informed them that he had failed to solve the mystery. So they said, "What shall we do now? How shall we catch him? Who will watch to-morrow?" A old buffaloe cow replied, "I will accept the responsibility." Hearing her speak thus the others said, "What a good elephant and a good horse could not do, will ten asses accomplish?" By this they meant, that two of the strongest of their number having failed, this weak old cow could not possibly succeed. However, she persisted, and in the morning the others went to graze leaving her behind.

In a short time she saw Jhore emerge from the dunghill, in which he resided, and loose the calves, and take them to the water. When he brought them back he cleaned and swept their stall, and then re-entered the dunghill. In the evening the others enquired, "Well, did you see him?" The old buffaloe cow replied, "Yes, I saw him, but I will not tell you, for you will kill him." They pressed her, but she refused, saying, "You will kill him." They said, "Why should we kill him who takes so much care of our young ones?" The old buffaloe cow led them to the dunghill, and said, "He is in here." So they called to him to come out, which he did, and when they saw him they were all greatly pleased, so much so that they there and then hired him to continue to do the work he had been doing so well. They arranged also to give him a regular daily supply of milk, so he was duly installed by the herd of wild buffaloes as care-taker of their calves.

Long after this, he one day took his calves to the river and after he had bathed them he said to the buffaloe calves, "Wait for me till I also bathe." They replied, "Bathe, we will graze close by." He having performed his ablutions sat down on the river bank to comb and dress his hair, which was twelve cubits long. In combing his tangled tresses a quantity was wrenched out, this he wrapped up in a leaf and threw into the stream. It was carried by the current a great distance down to where a raja's daughter and her companions were bathing. The raja's daughter saw the leaf floating towards her, and ordered one of her attendants to bring it to her. When the leaf was opened it was found to contain hair twelve cubits in length. Immediately after measuring the hair the raja's daughter complained of fever, and hasted home to her couch. The raja being informed of his daughter's illness sent for the most skilled physicians, who prescribed all the remedies their pharmacopœia contained, but failed to afford the sufferer any relief. The grief of the raja was therefore intense.

Then his daughter said to him, "Oh! father, I have one word to say to you. If you do as I wish, I shall recover." The raja replied, "Tell me what it is, I shall do my best to please you." So she said, "If you find me one with hair twelve cubits long and bring him to me, I shall rally at once." The raja said, "It is well."

The raja caused diligent search to be made for the person with hair twelve cubits long. He said to a certain jugi, "You traverse the country far and near, find me the man with hair twelve cubits long." The jugi enquired everywhere, but could obtain no intelligence concerning him.

They then made up a parcel of flour and gave it to a crow, whom they sent to try and find him. The crow flew caw cawing all over the district, but returned at last and reported failure, saying, "there is not such a man in the world."

After this they again made up a small parcel of flour, and giving it to a tame paroquet, said, "Find a man with hair twelve cubits long." The paroquet, having received his orders, flew away screeching, and mounting high up into the sky, directed his course straight for the unexplored forest. In the meantime the dunghill in which Jhore resided had become a palace.

The paroquet alighted on a tree near Jhore's palace, and began to whistle. On hearing the unusual sound Jhore came out and saw the paroquet who was speaking and whistling. The paroquet also eyed him narrowly, and was delighted to see his hair trailing on the ground. By this he knew that he had found the object of his search, and with a scream of delight, he flew away to communicate the tidings to the raja.

The raja was overjoyed with his messenger's report, and ordered the *bariat* to set out immediately. In a short time they were on their way accompanied by elephants, horses, drums, and fifes. On reaching Jhore's palace they were about to enter for the purpose of seizing him, when he exclaimed, "Do not pass my threshold." They replied, "We will carry you away with us." He said, "Do not come near." "We will certainly carry you away," they replied. Jhore then ran into his house, and seizing his flute mounted to the roof, and began to play. As the notes of the flute resounded through the forest it seemed to say,

A staff of Pader1 wood

A flute of Erandom2

Return, return, return,

Oh! wild buffaloe cows.

The sound of the flute startled the wild buffaloes, and they said one to another, "Sister. What has happened to Jhore?" Then he played again the same as before;

A staff of Pader wood

A flute of Erandom

Return, return, return,

Oh! wild buffaloe cows.

As the echoes of Jhore's flute died away in the forest glades the wild buffaloes sprang forward, and rushed to his assistance. On arrival they found the house and courtyard full of people, and large numbers outside who could not gain admittance. They immediately charged them with all their force, goring many to death, and scattering the remainder, who flung away their drums and fifes, and fled as for dear life.

When the raja heard of their discomfiture he sent again for the paroquet, and giving a small parcel of flour to him said, "Stay some time with him until you gain his confidence, and watch your chance to bring away his flute." Having received his orders he flew off to Jhore's palace, and having gained access to where the flute was, when Jhore was out of the way he brought it away, and gave it to the raja. The raja was delighted at the sight of the flute, and again ordered the *bariat* to go to fetch Jhore. A still more imposing array than the former started with elephants, horses, drums, fifes, and palkis, and in due course arrived at Jhore's residence. On seeing them Jhore called out, "Do not approach, or you will rue it presently." They replied, "You beat us off the first time, therefore you now crow, but you will not now be able to balk us, we shall take you with us." Again he warned them to stay where they were, saying, "Do not come near me, or you will rue it presently." They replied, "We will take you with us this time, we will not leave you behind." Jhore then ran into his house, and searched for his flute, but as it had been carried away by the paroquet he could not find it, so seizing another he mounted to the roof, and began to play. The flute seemed to say;

A staff of Pader wood

A flute of Erandom
Return, return, return,
Oh! wild buffaloe cows.

The sound startled the wild buffaloes who said one to another "Sister. What is it Jhore says?" Again the music of the flute reached their ears, and the entire herd rushed off to Jhore's rescue. They charged the crowd in and around the palace of their favourite with such determination that in a few minutes many lay gored to death, and those who were so fortunate as to escape threw down drums, fifes, and palkis, and fled pell mell from the place. The raja, being informed of the catastrophe that had befallen the *bariat*, again called the paroquet, and after he had given him careful instructions as to how he should proceed, dismissed him. He said, "This time you must stay many days with him, and secure his entire confidence and friendship. Then you must bring away all his flutes, do not leave him one." So the paroquet flew swiftly, and alighted on a tree near to Jhore's house, and began to whistle. Jhore seeing it was a paroquet brought it food, and induced it to come down, and allow him to take it in his hand. The two, it is said, lived together many days, and greatly enjoyed each other's society. The paroquet when he had informed himself as to where all Jhore's flutes were kept, one day tied them all up in a bundle, and carried them to the raja. The sight of the flutes revived the drooping spirits of his Majesty. He gave orders a third time for the *bariat* to go and bring Jhore, so they started with greater pomp and show than before. Elephants, horses, and an immense number of men with drums and fifes, and palkis formed the procession. On their arrival Jhore came out of his palace and said to them, "Do not come near, or you will rue it." They replied, "This time we will have you. We will take you with us." Again Jhore warning them said, "Come no nearer. If you do, you will see something as good as a show. Do you not remember how you fared the other day?" But they said, "We will carry you away with us." Jhore ran inside to get his flute, so that he might call the wild buffaloes to his assistance; but no flute was to be found. Without the help of his powerful friends he could offer no resistance, so they seized him, and bore him away in triumph to the raja.

When the raja's daughter heard of his arrival the fever suddenly left her, and she was once more in excellent health. She and Jhore were united in the bonds of marriage forthwith; but Jhore was kept a close prisoner in the palace.

In course of time a son blessed the union, and when the child was able to walk Jhore's wife said to him, "Where is the large herd of buffaloes which you boast so much about? If they were here "Sonny" would have milk and curds daily." Jhore plucking up courage, replied, "If you do not believe me order a stockade to be constructed thirty-two miles long and thirty-two miles broad, and you shall soon behold my buffaloes." So they made a pen thirty-two miles long and thirty-two miles broad. Then Jhore said, "Give me my old flute, and you all remain within doors." So they brought him his flute, and he went up on to the roof of the palace, and played. The music seemed to call as follows:

A staff of Pader wood

A flute of Erandom

Return, return, return,

Oh! wild buffaloe cows.

The sound startled the wild buffaloes in their forest home, and they said one to another, "Sister. What does Jhore say?" Again the music seemed to say,

A staff of Pader wood

A flute of Erandom

Return, return, return,

Oh! wild buffaloe cows.

At Jhore's second call the herd of wild buffaloes dashed off at their utmost speed, and never halted till they reached the raja's palace. They came in such numbers that the pen could not contain them all, many remained outside.

Those that entered the pen are the domesticated buffaloes of to-day, and those who were without are the wild buffaloes still found in the forests of India.

1 Stereospermum suaveolens, D. C.

2 Recinus communis, Linn.

The Girl who always found helpers.

There were once upon a time, six brothers and a sister. The brothers were married. They were merchants, and their business often took them to a distance from home. On such occasions the wives were left alone with their sister-in-law. For some reason or other they hated the girl, and took every opportunity to harass and worry her.

One day when the brothers were away on a journey they said to her, "Oh! girl, go to the forest and bring a load of firewood without tying it." What could the girl do? She must obey her sisters-in-law, or else they would beat her, and give her no food. So she went to the forest with a heavy heart, bewailing her unhappy lot in the following plaintive song,

> Woe is me! For I must bring
> Unbound a fagot on my head.

> Oh! brothers dear, I weeping sing
> While business you far hence hath led.

Seeing her grief a Jambro snake asked, "Why daughter, do you cry?" She replied, "My brothers have gone away on business, and my sisters-in-law persecute me. They have sent me to bring a bundle of firewood on my head without tying it." The Jambro took pity on her and said, "Gather firewood." Then the Jambro stretched himself full length upon the ground and said to the girl, "Lay the sticks on me." When she had done so the serpent twined itself round the fagot like a rope, and said, "Now lift it on to your head, but when you reach home, lay your burden down gently."

When her sisters-in-law knew that she had done what they considered impossible, they were still more angry with her, and ordered her to go to the forest and get milk from a tigress. They gave her a small earthen vessel, saying, "Go, bring us the milk of a tigress." What could the girl do? She went to the forest with a heavy heart, bewailing her unhappy lot in the following plaintive song,

> Woe is me! For I must bring
> A brimful cup of tigress' milk
> Oh! brothers dear, I weeping sing

While you far hence by trade are lured.

She went to the tiger's den, but only found two cubs, who seeing her sitting weeping at the entrance said, "What are you seeking?" She replied, "My sisters-in-law have sent me to bring some of your mother's milk." The cubs took pity on her and hid her in the cave. They said to her, "Our mother will devour you, so you must not shew yourself." In a short time the tigress returned, and entering the den said, "I smell a human being. Where is he?" The cubs replied, "There is no one here." The cubs milked a little of their mother's milk into the girl's vessel, and when the way was clear they gave it to her, and sent her home.

Her sisters-in-law were greatly disappointed when she brought home the milk, they had expected that the tiger would have devoured her, on that she would return home empty handed, and so give them the opportunity of abusing her for not carrying out their order.

Another day when the brothers were absent they called her, and said, "Go to the forest and bring us some bear's milk." What could the girl do? If she did not do as she was bidden her sisters-in-law would beat her, and give her nothing to eat. So taking the vessel in her hand, she went to the forest, bewailing her unhappy lot in the following plaintive strains;

> Woe is me! For I must bring
>
> A brimful cup of she bear's milk
>
> Oh! brothers dear, I weeping sing
>
> While you far hence by trade are lured.

Going to the bear's den she sat down and wept. The she-bear was not in the den, only two cubs were there, who, when they saw the girl, took pity upon her, and asked why she wept. She replied, "My brothers have gone away on business, and my sisters-in-law, who hate me, have sent me to procure bear's milk in order to harass and annoy me." The bear cubs then said, "Our mother will eat you, if she finds you, so we will hide you, and you must keep quiet while she is here." The she-bear on entering the cave said, "I smell a human being." The cubs replied, "There is no one here." The young ones succeeded in obtaining a small quantity of their mother's milk in the girl's earthen vessel, and after the mother bear had left, the cubs dismissed her with their best wishes for her welfare.

Her sisters-in-law were extremely annoyed when she presented the bear's milk to them. They had expected that the bear would have torn her to pieces, or that she would have returned empty handed, and thus give them another chance to abuse and reproach her.

The girl's sisters-in-law again took advantage of their husbands' absence to send her to bring water from the spring in a water-pot with a hole in it. They said, "Go bring water in this water-pot." What could the girl do? She placed it on her head, and went towards the spring bewailing her unhappy lot in the following plaintive song,

Woe is me! For I must bring

Spring water in a leaking jar

Oh! brothers dear, I weeping sing

While business you far hence hath lured.

She seated herself near the well, and exclaimed, "How can I carry water in this pot?" At that moment a frog raised his head above the reeds, and said, "Why do you sit here lamenting?" The girl replied, "My sisters-in-law, who hate me, have ordered me to bring water in this pot which has a large hole in the bottom. How is it possible for me to obey their order?" The frog replied, "Do not worry yourself over it, I will help you." So he pressed himself tightly over the hole, and she filled her pot, and carried it home on her head.

Her sisters-in-law, when they saw her place the water-pot on the ground, full to the brim, were intensely mortified. They had looked for her returning with an empty pitcher, thus affording them an ostensible reason for maliciously upbraiding her.

Another time they scattered a large basketful of Mustard seed on the ground, and ordered her to pick up every seed. They said to her, "You must gather it all into the basket again." What could she do? If she failed they would beat her, entreat her spitefully, and deprive her of food. As she gazed upon the seeds scattered all around her, she bewailed her unhappy condition as follows:

Woe is me! I must refill

This basket with these scattered seeds

Oh! brothers dear, I weeping sing

While business you far hence hath lured.

The plaintive murmur of her song had scarcely died away when a large flock of pigeons alighted near her. They said, "Why do you weep?" She replied, "My sisters-in-law, who hate me, have scattered all this mustard seed on the ground, and have ordered me to pick it all up. One solitary seed must not be left." The pigeons said, "Do not vex yourself, we will soon pick it up for you." As the pigeons were very numerous they soon collected it all into the basket. They did not leave one seed on the ground.

When she called her sisters-in-law to come and see how efficiently the work had been done, they were furious at being again balked by her, and vowed vengeance.

Once again, when the brothers were from home, her sisters-in-law ordered her to go to the jungle, and bring a bale of leaves with which to make the family cups and plates. They said to her, "Go to the jungle and bring a large bale of leaves, but do so without in anyway tying them." What could the girl do? She had been ordered to perform an impossibility. If she refused, or failed to do it, her sisters-in-law would beat her, and deprive her of food. So she went to the forest bewailing her unhappy lot in the following plaintive song;

> Woe is me! For I must bring
>
> Of forest leaves an unbound bale
>
> Oh! brothers dear, I weeping sing
>
> While business you far hence hath lured.

As she was sitting in the forest weeping a Horhorang serpent drew near and said, "Wherefore daughter do you grieve?" She replied, "My sisters-in-law hate me and have ordered me to bring leaves without tying them into a bundle. I cannot do this, and I fear their resentment, so I cannot help weeping." The Horhorang said, "Vex not yourself. Go and pluck your leaves and bring them here." She did so, and the Horhorang twined himself round them binding them into a sheaf, which the girl placed upon her head, and carried home.

When her sisters-in-law saw the leaves, and had looked to see that none had fallen by the way they were greatly chagrined. They had expected an opportunity to reproach her with disobedience, and a reason for punishing her.

Although her sisters-in-law had imposed so many impossibilities upon her, yet they had been unable to defeat her. Just at the proper time some one had appeared to help her.

They had seen a bunch of flowers on the top of a high tree, and one day when their husbands were away, they said to her, "Climb up into the tree and pluck the flowers, we wish to dress our hair with them on the occasion of your marriage." No sooner had she clambered up into the tree than her sisters-in-law placed thorny bushes all round in such a manner as to prevent her coming down again. They then went home.

A few days afterwards, the brothers, when returning from a distant market to which they had gone rested for a little under this tree. A tear drop fell on the hand of one of them. Looking at it he said, "Look brothers, this tear drop resembles those of the daughter." Then they looked and saw her high up in the tree. They quickly brought her down, and she related how in time past she had been persecuted by her sisters-in-law whenever they were absent. The brothers were wroth with their wives for having used her so cruelly.

The brothers put their sister into a bag, and carried her home on a bullock's back. When the wives came out to welcome them, they asked, "Where is the daughter?" They gave no reply.

Afterwards the brothers dug a deep well, and on the pretence of propitiating the water spirit induced their wives to stand round the well with offerings of rice, &c., in their hands. At a given signal each hurled his wife head foremost into the well. They then placed a cart over the opening.

In return for the persecution she had endured at their hands, the girl used to go to the well and looking in, say, "You treated me cruelly once, but now, boo sisters boo."

A Simple Thief.

Once upon a time a man had some money given to him, and was told to go and buy a foal with it. So he set out to search for one. After a time he came to a village, and going to a house asked the people if they had a foal to sell, as he wished to buy one. They replied, "There are no foals here, but we have mare's eggs. If you will take them we will give them to you." He said, "I will not take eggs, I want a foal." He went to every house in the village asking if they had a foal to sell, but none was to be had; but at each they offered to sell to him mare's eggs.

He then thought within himself, wherever I have gone they have told me that they have not got a foal, but that they can let me have eggs. This being so, why should I give myself any further trouble? I will buy an egg. So he was given a large gourd, and told it was a mare's egg. Having got, as he thought a mare's egg, he joyfully started to return to his home. The man who sold him the gourd informed him, that a foal was certain to be hatched on the way. He was still far from home when the sun set, so he entered a village, and passed the night there. In the morning he set out betimes, and about breakfast time he came to a tank, on the embankment of which he laid down his gourd. He then went into the water to clean his teeth, after which he began to wash his face. While he was thus engaged a jackal came and pushed the gourd down the embankment. The noise frightening the animal it ran away, but the man having caught a glimpse of it called out, "My foal has hatched, and is galloping off." He pursued the jackal, which being terror stricken fled to the jungle, and took refuge in his burrow. The man was pleased to see the creature enter his hole, and he said, "He will soon come out again, and then I shall mount him, and gallop him home." Having said this, he placed himself in such a position that when the jackal came out he could sit down on its back.

He continued standing thus until nightfall, but even then he had no intention of relinquishing his chance of capturing his foal. Late at night some thieves came that way, and seeing him alone in the jungle asked him what he did there. He replied, "I was sent by my friends to buy a foal, but as I could not get one, I bought a mare's egg. I was informed that the egg would hatch on my way home. I spent last night in a village on the way side, and resumed my homeward journey in the morning. On arriving at a tank I laid down my egg on the embankment, and went down into the water, and having cleaned my teeth was washing my hands and face, when the egg hatched and the foal immediately ran away. I followed it, and saw it enter this hole, and I am waiting till it comes out, when I shall mount, and canter it home."

The thieves said, "Leave it alone. Let it remain there. Will you kill yourself for this foal? Come with us, and we will give you a strong, beautiful horse. This one has through fear of you riding on his back gone into this hole. Why should you wait for him? He will stay where he is. Come with us, and we will supply you with a good one presently."

After a little time spent in considering the offer the thieves had made him, he decided to accompany them. The thieves were pleased to receive him into their gang, and at once they proceeded towards a certain village. Having arrived there they went to a rich man's house, and dug a hole through the wall. They then said to our hero of the mare's egg, "You creep in." He raised no objection, but went willingly. They said to him, "Bring out all the heavy articles you can find, they are sure to be the most valuable." When inside he lifted up all he found to test the weight, but nothing seemed to be sufficiently heavy to be worth stealing. He said, "everything is light, what can I take out to them?" At length he came across a millstone, which he pushed through the hole in the wall to his confederates out side. Judging from its weight he expected they would be delighted to receive it, but they said, "Not this, Not this. Bring something worth stealing." So he went back, and finding a drum hanging from the roof he took it down, and began to beat it. When the thieves heard the sound of the drum they decamped, saying, "This fool is certain to betray us to-night." When he brought out the drum to make it over to them, they were nowhere to be seen, so he re-entered the house and placed the drum again where he had found it.

He then saw some milk near the fireplace, and being hungry he determined to cook some food. So helping himself to some rice he began to prepare it by boiling it in the milk. When it was nearly cooked, one of the household turned over in his sleep, saying, "I will eat. I will eat." So he filled a ladle with the boiling rice and milk, and poured it into the sleeper's mouth. The hot food scalded him terribly, and he sprang up howling with the pain.

The other members of the family also jumped to their feet, and laid hold of the intruder, and bound him hand and foot.

When the day broke a large number of people came to see the thief, and began to question him, as to who were his companions. So he related all that had occurred. Then they said, "Of a truth, this man has been the means of protecting us. Had he not acted as he did, we would have been robbed of all we have."

So they loosed his bonds, and set him free. They also allowed him to eat the rice and milk he had cooked, which having done, he went home.